Mary Elizabeth Braddon

Henry Dunbar

Vol. 2

SALZWASSER
VERLAG

Mary Elizabeth Braddon

Henry Dunbar

Vol. 2

Reprint of the original, first published in 1864.

1st Edition 2022 | ISBN: 978-3-75259-396-9

Verlag (Publisher): Salzwasser Verlag GmbH, Zeilweg 44, 60439 Frankfurt, Deutschland
Vertretungsberechtigt (Authorized to represent): E. Roepke, Zeilweg 44, 60439 Frankfurt, Deutschland
Druck (Print): Books on Demand GmbH, In de Tarpen 42, 22848 Norderstedt, Deutschland

HENRY DUNBAR

THE STORY OF AN OUTCAST

BY THE AUTHOR OF

"LADY AUDLEY'S SECRET"

IN THREE VOLUMES

VOL. II.

FIFTH EDITION REVISED

LONDON

MDCCCLXIV.

CONTENTS OF VOL. II.

HENRY DUNBAR

CHAPTER I.

THREE WHO SUSPECT.

No further discovery was made respecting the murder that had been committed in the grove between Winchester and St. Cross. The police made every effort to find the murderer, but without result. A large reward was offered by the government for the apprehension of the guilty man; and a still larger reward was offered by Mr. Dunbar, who declared that his own honour and good name were in a manner involved in the discovery of the real murderer.

The one clue by which the police hoped to trace the footsteps of the assassin was the booty which his crime had secured to him: the contents of the pocket-book that had been rifled, and the clothes which had been stripped from the corpse of the victim. By means of the clue which these things might afford, the detective police hoped to reach the guilty man. But they hoped in vain. Every pawnbroker's shop in Winchester, and in every town within a certain radius of Winchester, was searched: but without effect. No clothes at all resembling those that had been seen upon the person of the dead man had been pledged within forty miles of the cathedral city. The police grew hopeless at last. The reward was a large one: but the darkness of the mystery seemed impenetrable, and little by little people left off talking of the murder. By slow degrees the gossips resigned themselves to the idea that the secret of Joseph Wilmot's death was to remain a secret for ever. Two or three "sensation" leaders appeared in some of the morning papers, urging the bloodhounds of the law to do their work, and taunting the members of the detective force with supineness and stupidity. I daresay the social leader-writers were rather hard-up for subjects at this stagnant autumnal period, and were scarcely sorry for the mysterious death of the man in the grove. The public grumbled a little when there was no new paragraph in the papers about "that dreadful Winchester murder;" but the nine-days' period during which the English public cares to wonder elapsed; and nothing had been done. Other murders were committed, as brutal in their nature as the murder in the grove: and the world, which rarely stops long to lament for the dead, began to think of other things. Joseph Wilmot was forgotten.

A month passed very quietly at Maudesley Abbey. Henry Dunbar took his place in the county as a person of importance; lights blazed in the splendid rooms; carriages drove in and out of the great gates in the park; and all the landed gentry within twenty miles of the abbey came to pay their respects to the millionaire who had newly returned from India. He did not particularly encourage people's visits; but he submitted himself to such festivities as his daughter declared to be necessary; and did the honours of his house with a certain haughty grandeur, which was a little stiff and formal as compared to the easy friendly grace of his high-bred visitors. People shrugged their shoulders, and hinted that there was something of the "roturier" in Mr. Dunbar; but they freely acknowledged that he was a fine handsome-looking fellow, and that his daughter was an angel, rendered still more angelic by the earthly advantage of half a million or so for her marriage-portion.

Meanwhile Margaret Wilmot lived alone in her simple countrified lodging, and thought sadly enough of the father whom she had lost.

He had not been a good father: but she had loved him nevertheless. She had pitied him for his sorrows, and the wrongs that had been done him. She had loved him for those feeble traces of a better nature that had been dimly visible in his character.

"He had not been *always* a cheat and a reprobate," the girl thought, as she sat pondering upon her father's fate. "He never would have been dishonest but for Henry Dunbar."

She remembered with bitter feelings the aspect of the rich man's house in Portland Place. She had caught a glimpse of its splendour upon the night after her return from Winchester. Through the narrow opening between the folding-doors she had seen the pictures and the statues glimmering in the lamp-light of the inner hall. She had seen in that brief moment a bright confusion of hot-house flowers, and trailing satin curtains, gilded mouldings, and frescoed panels, the first few shallow steps of a marble staircase, the filigree-work of the bronze balustrade.

Only for one moment had she peeped wonderingly into the splendid interior of Henry Dunbar's mansion: but the objects seen in that one brief glance had stamped themselves upon the girl's memory.

"He is rich," she thought, "and they say that wealth can buy all the best things upon this earth. But, after all, there are few *real* things that it can purchase. It can buy flattery, and simulated love, and sham devotion: but it cannot buy one genuine heart-throb, one thrill of true feeling. All the wealth of this world cannot buy *peace* for Henry Dunbar, or forgetfulness. So long as I live, he shall be made to remember. If his own guilty conscience can suffer him to forget, it shall be my task to recall the past. I promised my dead father that I would remember the name of Henry Dunbar: I have had good reason to remember it."

Margaret Wilmot was not quite alone in her sorrow. There was one person who sympathised with her, with an earnest and pure desire to help her in her sorrow. This person was Clement Austin, the cashier in St. Gundolph's Lane; the man who had fallen head-over-heels in love with the pretty music-mistress, but who felt half ashamed of his sudden and unreasoning affection.

"I have always ridiculed what people call 'love at sight,'" he thought; "surely I am not so silly as to have been bewitched by hazel eyes and a straight nose. Perhaps, after all, I only take an interest in this girl because she is so beautiful and so lonely, and because of the kind of mystery there seems to be about her life."

Never for one moment had Clement Austin

suspected that this mystery involved any thing discreditable to Margaret herself. The girl's sad face seemed softly luminous with the tender light of pure and holy thoughts. The veriest churl could scarcely have associated vice or falsehood with such a lovely and harmonious image.

Since her return from Winchester, since the failure of her second attempt to see Henry Dunbar, her life had pursued its wonted course; and she went so quietly about her daily duties, that it was only by the settled sadness of her face, the subdued gravity of her manner, that people became aware of some heavy grief that had newly fallen upon her.

Clement Austin had watched her far too closely not to understand her better than other people. He had noticed the change in her costume, when she put on simple inexpensive mourning for her dead father; and he ventured to express his regret for the loss which she had experienced. She told him, with a gentle sorrowful accent in her voice, that she had lately lost someone who was very dear to her; and that the loss had been unexpected, and was very bitter to bear. But she told him no more: and he was too well bred to intrude upon her grief by any further question.

But though he refrained from saying more upon this occasion, the cashier brooded long and deeply upon the conduct of his niece's music-mistress: and one chilly September evening, when Miss Wentworth was *not* expected at Clapham, he walked across Wandsworth Common, and went straight to the lane in which Godolphin Cottages sheltered themselves under the shadow of the sycamores.

Margaret had very few intervals of idleness, and there was a kind of melancholy relief to her in such an evening as this; on which she was free to think of her dead father, and the strange story of his death. She was standing at the low wooden gate opening into the little garden below the window of her room, in the deepening twilight of this September evening. It was late in the month: the leaves were falling from the trees, and drifting with a rustling sound along the dusty roadway.

The girl stood with her elbow resting upon the top of the gate, and a dark shawl covering her head and shoulders. She was tired and unhappy, and she stood in a melancholy attitude, looking with sad eyes towards the glimpse of the river at the bottom of the lane. So entirely was she absorbed by her own gloomy thoughts, that she did not hear a footstep approaching from the other end of the lane; she did not look up until a man's voice said, in subdued tones—

"Good evening, Miss Wentworth; are you not afraid of catching cold? I hope your shawl is thick, for the dews are falling, and here, near the river, there is a damp mist on these autumn nights."

The speaker was Clement Austin.

Margaret Wilmot looked up at him, and a pensive smile stole over her face. Yes, it was something to be spoken to so kindly in that deep manly voice. The world had seemed so blank since her father's death: such utter desolation had descended upon her since her miserable journey to Winchester, and her useless visit to Portland Place: for since that time she had shrunk away from people, wrapped in her own sorrow, separated from the commonplace world by the exceptional nature of her misery. It was something to this poor girl to hear thoughtful and considerate words; and the unbidden tears clouded her eyes.

As yet she had spoken openly of her trouble to no living creature, since that night upon which she had attempted to gain admission to Mr. Dunbar's house. She was still known in the neighbourhood as Margaret Wentworth. She had put on mourning; and she had told the few people about the place where she lived, of her father's death: but she had told no one the manner of that death. She had shared her gloomy secret with neither friends nor counsellors, and had borne her dismal burden alone. It was for this reason that Clement Austin's friendly voice raised an unwonted emotion in her breast. The desolate girl remembered that night upon which she had first heard of the murder, and she remembered the sympathy that Mr. Austin had evinced on that occasion.

"My mother has been quite anxious about you, Miss Wentworth," said Clement Austin. "She has noticed such a change in your manner for the last month or five weeks; though you are as kind as ever to my little niece, who makes wonderful progress under your care. But my mother cannot be indifferent to your own feelings, and she and I have both perceived the change. I fear there is some great trouble on your mind; and I would give much—ah, Miss Wentworth, you cannot guess how much!—if I could be of help to you in any time of grief or trouble. You seemed very much agitated by the news of that shocking murder at Winchester. I have been thinking it all over since, and I cannot help fancying that the change in your manner dated from the evening on which my mother told you that dreadful story. It struck me, that you must, therefore, in some way or other, be interested in the fate of the murdered man. Even beyond this, it might be possible that, if you knew this Joseph Wilmot, you might be able to throw some light upon his antecedents, and thus give a clue to the assassin. Little by little this idea has crept into my mind, and to-night I resolved to come to you, and ask you the direct question, as to whether you were in any way related to this unhappy man."

At first Margaret Wilmot's only answer was a choking sob; but she grew calmer presently, and said, in a low voice—

"Yes, you have guessed rightly, Mr. Austin; I was related to that most unhappy man. I will tell you every thing; but not here," she added, looking back at the cottage windows, in which lights were glimmering; "the people about me are inquisitive, and I don't want to be overheard."

She wrapped her shawl more closely round her, and went out of the little garden. She walked by Clement's side down to the pathway by the river, which was lonely enough at this time of the night.

Here she told him her story. She carefully suppressed all vehement emotion; and in few and simple words related the story of her life.

"Joseph Wilmot was my father," she said. "Perhaps he may not have been what the world calls a good father; but I know that he loved me, and he was very dear to me. My mother was the daughter of a gentleman, a post-captain in the Royal Navy, whose name was Talbot. She met my father at the house of a lady from whom she used to receive music-lessons. She did not know who he was, or what he was. She only knew that he called himself James Wentworth; but he loved her, and she returned his affection. She was very young—a mere child, who had not long emerged from a boarding-school—and she married my poor father in defiance of the advice of her friends. She ran away from her home one morning, was married by stealth in an obscure little church in the City, and then went home with my father to confess what she had done. Her father never forgave her for that secret marriage. He swore that he would never look upon her face after that day: and he never did, until he saw it in her coffin. At my mother's death Captain Talbot's heart was touched: he came for the first time to my father's house, and offered to take me away with him, and to have me brought up amongst his younger children. But my father refused to allow this. He grieved passionately for my poor mother: though I have heard him say that he had much to regret in his conduct towards her. But I can scarcely remember that sad time. From that period our life became a wandering and wretched one. Sometimes, for a little while, we seemed better off. My father got some employment; he worked steadily; and we lived amongst respectable people. But soon—ah, cruelly soon!—the new chance of an honest life was taken away from him. His employers heard something: a breath, a whisper, perhaps: but it was enough. He was not a man to be trusted. He promised well: so far he had kept his promise: but there was a risk in employing him. My father never met any good Christian who was willing to run that risk, in the hope of saving a human soul. My father never met any one noble enough to stretch out his hand to the outcast, and say, 'I know that you have done wrong; I know that you are without a character: but I will forget the blot upon the past, and help you to achieve redemption in the future.' If my father had met such a friend, such a benefactor, all might have been different."

Then Margaret Wilmot related the substance

of the last conversation between herself and her father. She told Clement Austin what her father had said about Henry Dunbar: and she showed him the letter which was directed to Norfolk Island—that letter in which the old clerk alluded to the power that his brother possessed over his late master. She also told Mr. Austin how Henry Dunbar had avoided her at Winchester and in Portland Place, and of the letter which he had written to her,—a letter in which he had tried to bribe her to silence.

"Since that night," she added, "I have received two anonymous enclosures,—two envelopes containing notes to the amount of a hundred pounds, with the words 'From a True Friend' written across the flap of the envelope. I returned both the enclosures; for I knew whence they had come. I returned them in two envelopes directed to Henry Dunbar, at the office in St. Gundolph's Lane."

Clement Austin listened with a grave face. All this certainly seemed to hint at the guilt of Mr. Dunbar. No clue pointing to any other person had been as yet discovered, though the police had been indefatigable in their search.

Mr. Austin was silent for some minutes; then he said, quietly—

"I am very glad you have confided in me, Miss Wilmot, and, believe me, you shall not find me slow to help you whenever my services can be of any avail. If you will come and drink tea with my mother at eight o'clock to-morrow evening, I will be at home; and we can talk this matter over seriously. My mother is a clever woman, and I know that she has a most sincere regard for you. You will trust her, will you not?"

"Willingly, with my whole heart."

"You will find her a true friend."

They had returned to the little garden-gate by this time. Clement Austin stretched out his hand.

"Good night, Miss Wilmot."

"Good night."

Margaret opened the gate and went into the garden. Mr. Austin walked slowly homewards, past pleasant cottages nestling in suburban gardens, and pretentious villas, with campanello-towers and gothic porches. The lighted windows shone out upon the darkness. Here and there he heard the sound of a piano, or a girlish voice stealing softly out upon the cool night air.

The sight of pleasant homes made the cashier think very mournfully of the girl he had just left.

"Poor, desolate girl," he thought—"poor, lonely, orphan girl!"

But he thought still more about that which he had heard of Henry Dunbar: and the evidence against the rich man seemed to grow in importance as he reflected upon it. It was not one thing, but many things, that hinted at the guilt of the millionaire.

The secret possessed, and no doubt traded upon, by Joseph Wilmot; Mr. Dunbar's agitation in the cathedral; his determined refusal to see the murdered man's daughter; his attempt to bribe her—these were strong points: and by the time Clement Austin reached home, he—like Margaret Wilmot, and like Arthur Lovell—suspected the millionaire. So now there were three people who believed Mr. Dunbar to be the murderer of his old servant.

CHAPTER II.

LAURA DUNBAR'S DISAPPOINTMENT.

ARTHUR LOVELL went often to Maudesley Abbey. Henry Dunbar welcomed him freely, and the young man had not the power to resist temptation. He went to his doom as the foolish moth flies to the candle. He went, he saw Laura Dunbar, and spent hour after hour in her society: for his presence was always agreeable to the impetuous girl. To her he seemed, indeed, that which he had promised to be, a brother—kind, devoted, affectionate: but no more. He was endeared to Laura by the memory of a happy childhood. She was grateful to him, and she loved him: but only as she would have loved him, had he been indeed her brother. Whatever deeper feeling lay beneath the playful gaiety of her manner had yet to be awakened.

So, day after day, the young man bowed down before the goddess of his life, and was happy—ah, fatally happy!—in her society. He forgot every thing except the beautiful face that smiled on him. He forgot even those dark doubts which he had felt as to the secret of the Winchester murder.

Perhaps he would scarcely have forgotten the suspicions that had entered his mind after the first interview between the banker and his daughter, had he seen much of Henry Dunbar. But he saw very little of the master of Maudesley Abbey. The rich man took possession of the suite of apartments that had been prepared for him, and rarely left his own rooms: except to wander alone amongst the shady avenues of the park: or to ride out upon the powerful horse he had chosen from the stud purchased by Percival Dunbar.

This horse was a magnificent creature; the colt of a thorough-bred sire, but of a stronger and larger build than a purely thorough-bred animal. He was a chestnut horse, with a coat that shone like satin, and not a white hair about him. His nose was small, his eyes large, his ears and neck long. He had all the points which an Arab prizes in his favourite barb.

To this horse Henry Dunbar became singularly attached. He had a loose box built on purpose for the animal in a private garden adjoining his own dressing-room, which, like the rest of his apartments, was situated upon the ground-floor of the abbey. Mr. Dunbar's groom slept in a part of the house near this loose box; and horse and man were at the service of the banker at any hour of the day or night.

Henry Dunbar generally rode either early in the morning, or in the gray twilight after his dinner-hour. He was a proud man, and he was not a sociable man. When the county gentry came to welcome him to England, he received them, and thanked them for their courtesy. But there was something in his manner that repelled rather than invited friendship. He gave one great dinner-party soon after his arrival at Maudesley; a ball, at which Laura floated about in a cloud of white gauze, and with diamonds in her hair; and a breakfast and morning concert on the lawn, in compliance with the urgent entreaties of the same young lady. But when invitations came flooding in upon Mr. Dunbar, he declined them one after another, on the ground of his weak health. Laura might go where she liked, always provided that she went under the care of a suitable chaperone; but the banker declared that the state of his health altogether unfitted him for society. His constitution had been much impaired, he said, by his long residence in Calcutta.

And yet he looked a strong man. Tall, broad-chested, and powerful, it was very difficult to perceive in Henry Dunbar's appearance any one of the usual evidences of ill-health. He was very pale: but that unchanging pallor was the only sign of the malady from which he suffered.

He rose early, rode for a couple of hours upon his chestnut horse Dragon, and then breakfasted. After breakfast he sat in his luxurious sitting-room, sometimes reading, sometimes writing, sometimes sitting for hours together brooding silently over the low embers in the roomy fire-place. At six o'clock he dined, still keeping to his own room—for he was not well enough to dine with his daughter, he said: and he sat alone late into the night, drinking heavily, according to the report current in the servants' hall.

He was respected and he was feared in his household: but he was not liked. His silent and reserved manner had a gloomy influence upon the servants who came in contact with him: and they compared him very disadvantageously with his predecessor, Percival Dunbar: the genial, kind, old master, who had always had a cheerful, friendly word for every one of his dependents: from the stately housekeeper, in rustling silken robes, to the smallest boy employed in the stables.

No, the new master of the abbey was not liked. Day after day he lived secluded and alone. At first, his daughter had broken in upon his solitude, and, with bright, caressing ways, had tried to win him from his loneliness: but she found that all her efforts to do this were worse than useless: they were even disagreeable to her father: and, by degrees, her light footstep was heard less and less often in that lonely wing of the house where Henry Dunbar had taken up his abode.

Maudesley Abbey was a large and rambling old mansion, which had been built in half-a-dozen different reigns. The most ancient part of the building was that very northern wing which Mr. Dunbar had chosen for himself. Here the architecture belonged to the early Plantagenet era; the stone walls were thick and massive, the lancet-headed windows were long and narrow, and the arms of the early benefactors of the monastery were emblazoned here and there upon the richly stained glass. The walls were covered with faded tapestry, from which grim faces scowled upon the lonely inhabitant of the chambers. The groined ceiling was of oak, that had grown black with age. The windows of Mr. Dunbar's bed-room and dressing-room opened into a cloistered court, beneath whose solemn shadow the hooded monks had slowly paced, in days that were long gone. The centre of this quadrangular court had been made into a garden, where tall hollyhocks and prim dahlias flaunted in the autumn sunshine.

And within this cloistered courtway Mr. Dunbar had erected the loose box for his favourite horse.

The southern wing of Maudesley Abbey owed its origin to a much later period. The windows and fire-places at this end of the house were in the Tudor style; the polished oak wainscoting was very beautiful; the rooms were smaller and snugger than the tapestried chambers occupied by the banker; Venetian glasses and old crystal chandeliers glimmered and glittered against the sombre woodwork; and elegant modern furniture contrasted pleasantly with the Elizabethan casements and carved oaken chimney-pieces. Every thing that unlimited wealth can do to make a house beautiful had been done for this part of the mansion by Percival Dunbar; and had been done with considerable success. The doting grandfather had taken a delight in beautifying the apartments occupied by his girlish companion: and Miss Dunbar had walked upon velvet pile, and slept beneath the shadow of satin curtains, from a very early period of her existence.

She was used to luxury and elegance: she was accustomed to be surrounded by all that is refined and beautiful: but she had that inexhaustible power of enjoyment which is perhaps one of the brightest gifts of a fresh young nature: and she did not grow tired of the pleasant home that had been made for her.

Laura Dunbar was a pampered child of fortune: but there are some natures that it seems very difficult to spoil: and I think hers must have been one of these.

She knew no weariness of the "rolling hours." To her the world seemed a paradise of beauty. Remember, she had never seen real misery: she had never endured that sick feeling of despair, which creeps over the most callous of us when we discover the amount of hopeless misery that is, and has been, and is to be, for ever and ever upon this weary earth. She had seen sick cottagers, and orphan children, and desolate widows, in her pilgrimages amongst the dwellings of the poor: but she had always been able to relieve these afflicted ones, and to comfort them more or less.

It is the sight of sorrows which we cannot alleviate that sends a palpable stab home to our hearts, and for a time almost sickens us with a universe which cannot go upon its course *without* such miseries as these.

To Laura Dunbar the world was still entirely beautiful, for the darker secrets of life had not been revealed to her.

Only once had affliction come near her; and then it had come in a calm and solemn shape, in the death of an old man, who ended a good and prosperous life peacefully upon the breast of his beloved granddaughter.

Perhaps her first real trouble came to her now in the bitter disappointment which had succeeded her father's return to England. Heaven only knows with what a tender yearning the girl had looked forward to Henry Dunbar's return. They had been separated for the best part of her brief lifetime: but what of that? He would love her all the more tenderly because of those long years during which they had been divided. She meant to be the same to her father that she had been to her grandfather—a loving companion, a ministering angel.

But it was never to be. Her father, by a hundred tacit signs, rejected her affection. He had shunned her presence from the first: and she had grown now to shun him. She told Arthur Lovell of this unlooked-for sorrow.

"Of all the things I ever thought of, Arthur, this never entered my head," she said, in a low, pensive voice, as she stood one evening in the deep embrasure of the Tudor window, looking thoughtfully out at the wide-spreading lawn, where the shadows of the low cedar branches made patches of darkness on the moonlit surface of the grass; "I thought that papa might fall ill on the voyage home, and die, and that the ship, for whose safe course I prayed night and day, might bring me nothing but the sacred remains of the dead. I have thought this, Arthur, and I have lain awake at night torturing myself with the thought: till my mind has grown so full of the dark picture, that I have seen the little cabin in the cruel, restless ship, and my father lying helpless on a narrow bed, with only strangers to watch his death-hour. I cannot tell you how many different things I have feared: but I never, never thought that he would not love me. I have even thought that it was just possible he might be unlike my grandfather, and a little unkind to me sometimes when I vexed or troubled him: but I thought his heart would be true to me through all, and that even in his harshest moments he would love me dearly, for the sake of my dead mother."

Her voice broke, and she sobbed aloud: but the man who stood by her side had no word of comfort to say to her. Her complaint awoke that old suspicion which had lately slumbered in his breast—the horrible fear that Mr. Dunbar was guilty of the murder of his old servant.

The young lawyer was bound to say something, however. It was too cruel to stand by and utter no word of comfort to this sobbing girl.

"Laura, dear Laura," he said, "this is foolish, believe me. You must have patience, and still hope for the best. How *can* your father do otherwise than love you, when he grows to know you well?

You may have expected too much of him. Remember, that people who have lived long in the East Indies are apt to become cold and languid in their manners. When Mr. Dunbar has seen more of you, when he has become better accustomed to your society—"

"That he will never be," Laura answered, impetuously. "How can he ever know me better when he scrupulously avoids me? Sometimes whole days pass during which I do not see him. Then I summon up courage and go to his dreary rooms. He receives me graciously enough, and treats me with politeness. With politeness! when I am yearning for his affection: and I linger a little perhaps, asking him about his health, and trying to get more at home in his presence. But there is always a nervous restlessness in his manner: which tells me,—oh, too plainly!—that my presence is unwelcome to him. So I go away at last, half heart-broken. I remember, now, how cold and brief his letters from India always seemed: but then he used to excuse himself to me upon account of the hurry of business: and he seldom finished his letter without saying that he looked joyfully forward to our meeting. It was very cruel of him to deceive me!"

Arthur Lovell was a sorry comforter. From the first he had tried in vain to like Henry Dunbar. Since that strange scene in Portland Place, he had suspected the banker of a foul and treacherous murder,—that worst and darkest crime; which for ever separates a man from the sympathy of his fellow-men, and brands him as an accursed and abhorred creature, beyond the pale of human compassion. Ah, how blessed is that Divine and illimitable compassion which can find pity for those whom sinful man rejects!

CHAPTER III.

NEW HOPES MAY BLOOM.

JOCELYN'S ROCK was ten miles from Maudesley Abbey, and only one mile from the town of Shorncliffe. It was a noble place, and had been in the possession of the same family ever since the days of the Plantagenets.

The house stood upon a rocky cliff, beneath which rushed a cascade that leapt from crag to crag, and fell into the bosom of a deep stream, that formed an arm of the river Avon. This cascade was forty feet below the edge of the cliff upon which the mansion stood.

It was not a very large house; for most of the older part of it had fallen into ruin long ago, and the ruined towers and shattered walls had been cleared away: but it was a noble mansion notwithstanding.

One octagonal tower, with a battlemented roof, still stood almost as firmly as it had stood in the days of the early Plantagenets, when rebel soldiers had tried the strength of their battering-rams against the grim stone walls. The house was built entirely of stone; the Gothic porch was ponderous as the porch of a church. Within all was splendour; but splendour that was very different from the modern elegance that was to be seen in the rooms of Maudesley Abbey.

At Jocelyn's Rock the stamp of age was upon every decoration, on every ornament. Square-topped helmets that had been hacked by the scimitars of Saracen kings, spiked chamfronts that had been worn by the fiery barbs of haughty English crusaders, fluted armour from Milan, hung against the blackened wainscoting in the shadowy hall; Scottish hackbuts, primitive arquebuses that had done service on Bosworth field, Homeric bucklers and brazen greaves, javelins, crossbows, steel-pointed lances, and two-handed swords, were in symmetrical design upon the dark and polished panels; while here and there hung the antlers of a giant red-deer, or the skin of a fox, in testimony to the triumphs of long-departed sportsmen of the house of Jocelyn.

It was a noble old house. Princes of the blood royal had sat in the ponderous carved oak-chairs. A queen had slept in the state-bed, in the blue-satin chamber. Loyal Jocelyns, fighting for their king against low-born Roundhead soldiers, had hidden themselves in the spacious chimneys: or had fled for their lives along the secret passages behind the tapestry. There were old pictures and jewelled drinking-cups that dead-and-gone Jocelyns had collected in the sunny land of the Medicis. There were costly toys of fragile Sèvres china that had been received by one of the earls from the hand of the lovely Pompadour herself in the days when the manufacturers of Sèvres only worked for their king, and were liable to fall a sacrifice to their art and their loyalty by the inhalation of arsenicated vapours. There was golden plate that a king had given to his proud young favourite in those feudal days when favourites were powerful in England. There was scarcely any object of value in the mansion that had not a special history attached to it, redounding to the honour and glory of the ancient house of Jocelyn.

And this splendid dwelling-place, rendered almost sacred by legendary associations and historical recollections, was now the property of a certain Sir Philip Jocelyn—a dashing young baronet, who had been endowed by nature with a handsome face, frank fearless eyes that generally had a smile in them, and the kind of manly figure which the late Mr. G. P. R. James was wont to designate stalwart; and who was moreover a crack shot, a reckless crosscountry-going rider, and a very tolerable amateur artist.

Sir Philip Jocelyn was not what is usually called an intellectual man. He was more warmly interested in a steeple-chase on Shorncliffe Common than in a pamphlet on political economy, even though Mr. Stuart Mill should himself be the author of the *brochure.* He thought John Scott a greater man that Maculloch; and Manton the gunmaker only second to Doctor Jenner as a benefactor of his race. He found the works of the late Mr. Apperly more entertaining than the last new Idyll from the pen of the Laureate; and was rather at a loss for small-talk when he found his feminine neighbour at a dinner-table was "deeply, darkly, beautifully blue." But the young baronet was by no means a fool, notwithstanding these sportsmanlike proclivities. The Jocelyns had been hard riders for half-a-dozen centuries or so, and crack shots ever since the invention of fire-arms. Sir Philip was a sportsman, but he did not "hunt in dreams," and he was prepared to hold his wife a great deal "higher than his horse," whenever he should win that pleasant addition to his household. As yet he had thought very little of the future Lady Jocelyn. He had a vague idea that he should marry, as the rest of the Jocelyns had married; and that he should live happily with his wife, as his ancestors had lived with their wives: with the exception of one dreadful man, called Hildebrande Jocelyn, who, at some remote and medieval period, had been supposed to throw his liege lady out of an oriel window that overhung the waterfall, upon the strength of an unfounded suspicion; and who afterwards, according to the legend, dug, or rather scooped, for himself a cave out of the cliff-side with no better tools than his own finger-nails, which he never cut after the unfortunate lady's foul murder. The legend went on further to state that the white wraith of the innocent victim might be seen, on a certain night in the year, rising out of the misty spray of the waterfall: but as nobody except one very weak-witted female Jocelyn had ever seen the vision, the inhabitants of the house upon the crag had taken so little heed of the legend that the date of the anniversary had come at last to be forgotten.

Sir Philip Jocelyn thought that he should marry "some of these days," and in the mean time troubled himself very little about the pretty daughters of country gentlemen whom he met now and again at races, and archery-meetings, and flower-shows, and dinner-parties, and hunting-balls, in the queer old town-hall at Shorncliffe. He was heart-whole; and looking out at life from the oriel-window of his dressing-room, whence he saw nothing but his own land, neatly enclosed in a ring-fence, he thought the world, about which some people made such dismal howling, was, upon the whole, an extremely pleasant place, containing very little that "a fellow" need complain of. He built himself a painting-room at Jocelyn's Rock; and whistled to himself for the hour together, as he stood before the easel, painting scenes in the hunting-field, or Arab horsemen whom he had met on the great flat sandy plains beyond Cairo, or brown-faced boys, or bright Italian peasant-girls; all sorts of pleasant objects, under cloudless skies of ultra-marine, with streaks of orange and vermilion to represent the sunset. He was not a great painter, nor indeed was there any element of greatness in his nature; but he painted as recklessly as he rode; his subjects were bright and cheerful; and his pictures were altogether of the order which unsophisticated people admire and call "pretty."

He was a very cheerful young man, and perhaps that cheerfulness was the greatest charm he possessed. He was a man in whom no force of fashion or companionship would ever engender the peevish blasé-ness so much affected by modern youth. Did he dance? Of course he did, and he adored dancing. Did he sing? Well, he did his best, and had a fine volume of rich bass voice, that sounded remarkably well on the water, after a dinner at the Star-and-Garter, in that dim dewy hour, when the willow-shadowed Thames is as a southern lake, and the slow dip of the oars is in itself a kind of melody. Had he been much abroad? Yes, and he gloried in the Continent; the dear old inconvenient inns, and the extortionate landlords, and the insatiable commissionaires—he revelled in the commissionaires; and the dear drowsy slow trains, with an absurd guard, who talks an unintelligible patois, and the other man, who always loses one's luggage! Delicious! And the dear little peasant-girls with white caps, who are so divinely pretty when you see them in the distance under a sunny meridian sky, and are so charming in coloured chalk upon tinted paper, but such miracles of ugliness, comparatively speaking, when you behold them at close quarters. And the dear jingling diligences, with very little harness to speak of, but any quantity of old rope; and the bad wines, and the dust, and the cathedrals, and the beggars, and the trente-et-quarante tables, and in short every thing. Sir Philip Jocelyn spoke of the universe as a young husband talks of his wife; and was never tired of her beauty or impatient of her faults.

The poor about Jocelyn's Rock idolised the young lord of the soil. The poor like happy people, if there is nothing insolent in their happiness. Philip was rich, and he distributed his wealth right royally: he was happy, and he shared his happiness as freely as he shared his wealth. He would divide a case of choice Manillas with a bed-ridden pensioner in the Union, or carry a bottle of the Jocelyn Madeira—the celebrated Madeira with the brown seal—in the pocket of his shooting-coat, to deliver it into the horny hands of some hard-working mother who was burdened with a sick child. He would sit for an hour together telling an agricultural labourer of the queer farming he had seen abroad; and he had stood godfather—by proxy—to half the yellow-headed urchins within ten-miles radius of Jocelyn's Rock. No taint of vice or dissipation had ever sullied the brightness of his pleasant life. No wretched country girl had ever cursed his name before she cast herself into the sullen waters of a lonely mill-stream. People loved him; and he deserved their love and was worthy of their respect. He had taken no high honours at Oxford; but the sternest officials smiled when they spoke of him, and recalled the boyish follies that were associated with his name; a sickly bedmaker had been pensioned for life by him; and the tradesmen who had served him testified to his merits as a prompt and liberal paymaster. I do not think that in all his life Philip Jocelyn had ever directly or indirectly caused a pang of pain or sorrow to any human being, unless it was, indeed, to a churlish heir-at-law, who may have looked with a somewhat evil eye upon the young man's vigorous and healthful aspect, which gave little hope to his possible successor.

The heir-at-law would have gnashed his teeth in impotent rage had he known the crisis which came to pass in the baronet's life a short time after

Mr. Dunbar's return from India; a crisis very common to youth, and very lightly regarded by youth: but a solemn and a fearful crisis notwithstanding.

The master of Jocelyn's Rock fell in love. All the poetry of his nature, all the best feelings, the purest attributes of an imperfect character, concentrated themselves into one passion. Sir Philip Jocelyn fell in love. The arch magician waved his wand, and all the universe was transformed into fairy land: a lovely Paradise, a modern Eden, radiant with the reflected light that it received from the face of a woman. I almost hesitate to tell this old, old story over again—this perpetual story of love at first sight.

It is very beautiful this sudden love, which is born of one glance at the wonderful face that has been created to bewitch us: but I doubt if it is not, after all, the baser form of the great passion. The love that begins with esteem, that slowly grows out of our knowledge of the loved one, is surely the purer and holier type of affection.

This love, whose gradual birth we rarely watch or recognise—this love, that steals on us like the calm dawning of the eastern light, strikes to a deeper root and grows into a grander tree than that fair sudden growth, that marvellous far-shooting butterfly-blossoming orchid, called love at first sight. The glorious exotic flower may be wanting: but the strong root lies deeply hidden in the heart.

The man who loves at first sight generally falls in love with the violet blue of a pair of tender eyes, the delicate outline of a Grecian nose. The man who loves the woman he has known and watched, loves her because he believes her to be the purest and truest of her sex.

To this last, love is faith. He cannot doubt the woman he adores: for he adores her because he believes and has proved her to be above all doubt. We may fairly conjecture that Othello's passion for the simple Venetian damsel was love at first sight. He loved Desdemona because she was pretty, and looked at him with sweet maidenly glances of pity when he told those prosy stories of his—with full traveller's license, no doubt—over Brabantio's mahogany.

The tawny-visaged general loved the old man's

daughter because he admired her, and not because he knew her: and so, by and by, on the strength of a few foul hints from a scoundrel, he is ready to believe this gentle, pitiful girl the basest and most abandoned of women.

Hamlet would not so have acted, had it been his fate to marry the woman he loved. Depend upon it, the Danish prince had watched Ophelia closely, and knew all the ins and outs of that young lady's temper, and had laid conversational traps for her occasionally, I daresay, trying to entice her into some bit of toadyism that should betray any latent taint of falsehood inherited from poor time-serving Polonius. The Prince of Denmark would have been rather a fidgety husband, perhaps: but he would never have had recourse to a murderous bolster, at the instigation of a low-born knave.

Unhappily, some women are apt to prefer passionate, blustering Othello to sentimental and metaphysical Hamlet. The foolish creatures are carried away by noise and clamour: and most believe him who protests the loudest.

Philip Jocelyn and Laura Dunbar met at that dinner-party which the millionaire gave to his friends in celebration of his return. They met again at the ball, where Laura waltzed with Philip; the young man had learned to waltz upon the other side of the Alps; and Miss Dunbar preferred him to any other of her partners. At the fête champêtre they met again; and had their future lives revealed to them by a theatrical-looking gipsy imported from London for the occasion, whose arch prophecies brought lovely blushes into Laura's cheeks, and afforded Philip an excellent opportunity for admiring the effect of dark-brown eyelashes drooping over dark-blue eyes. They met again and again; now at a steeple-chase, now at a dinner-party, where Laura appeared with some friendly chaperone; and the baronet fell in love with the banker's beautiful daughter.

He loved her truly and devotedly, after his own mad-headed fashion. He was a true Jocelyn—impetuous, mad-headed, daring: and from the time of those festivities at Maudesley Abbey, he only dreamed and thought of Laura Dunbar. From that hour he haunted the neighbourhood of Maudesley Abbey. There was a bridle-path through the park to a little village called Lisford: and if that primitive Warwickshire village had been the most attractive place upon this earth, Sir Philip could scarcely have visited it oftener than he did.

Heaven knows what charm he found in the shady slumberous old street, the low stone market-place, with rusty iron gates surmounted by the Jocelyn escutcheon. The grass grew in the quiet quadrangle: the square church-tower was half hidden by the sheltering ivy: the gabled cottage-roofs were lop-sided with age. It was scarcely a place to offer any very great attraction to the lord of Jocelyn Rock in all the glory of his early manhood: and yet Philip Jocelyn went there three times a-week upon an average, during the period that succeeded the ball and morning concert at Maudesley Abbey.

The shortest way from Jocelyn's Rock to Lisford was by the high road: but Philip Jocelyn did not care to go by the shortest way. He preferred to take that pleasant bridle-path through

Maudesley Park, that delicious grassy arcade where the overarching branches of the old elms made a shadowy twilight, only broken now and then by sudden patches of yellow sunshine: where the feathery ferns trembled with every low whisper of the autumn breeze: where there was a faint perfume of pine wood: where every here and there, between the lower branches of the trees, there was a blue glimmer of still water-pools, half-hidden under flat green leaves of wild aquatic plants: where there was a solemn stillness, that reminded one of the holy quiet of a church: and where Sir Philip Jocelyn had every chance of meeting with Laura Dunbar.

He met her there very often. Not alone, for Dora Macmahon was sometimes with her, and the faithful Elizabeth Madden was always at hand to play propriety, and to keep a sharp eye upon the interests of her young mistress. But then it happened unfortunately that the faithful Elizabeth was very stout, and rather asthmatic; and though Miss Dunbar could not have had a more devoted duenna, she might certainly have had a more active one. And it also happened that Miss Macmahon, having received several practical illustrations of the old adage with regard to the disadvantage of a party of three persons as compared to a party of two persons, fell into the habit of carrying her books with her, and would sit and read in some shady nook near the abbey, while Laura wandered into the wilder regions of the park.

Beneath the shelter of the overarching elms, amidst the rustling of the trembling ferns, Laura Dunbar and Philip Jocelyn met very often during that bright autumnal weather. Their meetings were purely accidental of course, as such meetings always are: but they were not the less pleasant because of their uncertainty.

They were all the more pleasant, perhaps. There was that delicious fever of suspense which kept both young eager hearts in a constant glow. There were Laura's sudden blushes, which made her wonderful beauty doubly wonderful. There was Philip Jocelyn's start of glad astonishment, and the bright sparkle in his dark-brown eyes, as he saw the slender, queenly figure approaching him under the shadow of the trees. How beautiful she looked, with the folds of her dress trailing over the dewy grass, and a flickering halo of sunlight tremulous upon her diadem of golden hair! Sometimes she wore a coquettish little hat, with a turned-up brim and a peacock's plume: sometimes a broad-leaved hat of yellow straw, with floating ribbons and a bunch of feathery grasses perched bewitchingly upon the brim. She had the dog Pluto with her always, and generally a volume of some new novel under her arm. I am ashamed to be obliged to confess that this young heiress was very frivolous, and liked reading novels better than improving her mind by the perusal of grave histories, or by the study of the natural sciences. She spent day after day in happy idleness—reading, sketching, playing, singing: talking sometimes gaily, sometimes seriously, to her faithful old nurse, or to Dora, or to Arthur Lovell, as the case might be. She had a thorough-bred horse that had been given to her by her grandfather, but she very rarely rode him beyond the grounds; for Dora Macmahon was no horsewoman, having been brought up by a prim aunt of her dead mother's, who looked upon riding as an unfeminine accomplishment; and Miss Dunbar had therefore no better companion for her rides than a gray-haired old groom, who had ridden behind Percival Dunbar for forty years or so.

Philip Jocelyn generally went to Lisford upon horseback; but when, as so often happened, he met Miss Dunbar and her companion strolling amongst the old elms, it was his habit to get off his horse, and to walk by Laura's side, leading the animal by the bridle. Sometimes he found the two young ladies sitting on a camp-stool at the foot of one of the trees, sketching effects of light and shadow in the deep glades around them. On such occasions the baronet used to tie his horse to the lower branch of an old elm, and taking his stand behind Miss Dunbar, would amuse himself by giving her a lesson in perspective, with occasional hints to Miss Macmahon, who, as the young man remarked, drew so much better than her sister, that she really required very little assistance.

By and by this began to be an acknowledged thing. Special hours were appointed for these artistic studies: and Philip Jocelyn ceased to go to Lisford at all, contenting himself with passing almost every fine morning under the elms at Maudesley. He found that he had a very intelligent pupil in the banker's daughter: but I think, if Miss Dunbar had been less intelligent, her instructor would have had patience with her, and would have still found his best delight beneath the shadow of those dear old elms.

What words can paint the equal pleasure of giving and receiving those lessons, in the art which was loved alike by pupil and master: but which was so small an element in the happiness of those woodland meetings? What words can describe Laura's pleading face when she found that the shadow of a ruined castle wouldn't agree with the castle itself, or that a row of poplars in the distance insisted on taking that direction which our transatlantic brothers call "slantindicular"? And then the cutting of pencils, and crumbling of bread, and searching for mislaid scraps of India-rubber, and mixing of water-colours, and adjusting of pallettes on the prettiest thumb in Christendom, or the planting a sheaf of brushes in the dearest little hand that ever trembled when it met the tenderly timid touch of an amateur drawing-master's fingers;—all these little offices, so commonplace and wearisome when a hard-worked and poorly-paid professor performs them for thirty or forty clamorous girls, on a burning summer afternoon, in a great dust-flavoured schoolroom with bare, curtainless windows, were in this case more delicious than any words of mine can tell.

But September and October are autumnal months: and their brightest sunshine is, after all, only a deceptive radiance when compared to the full glory of July. The weather grew too cold for the drawing-lessons under the elms, and there could be no more appointments made between Miss Dunbar and her enthusiastic instructor.

"I can't have my young lady ketch cold, Sir Philip, for all the perspectuses in the world," said the faithful Elizabeth. "I spoke to her par about it only the other day; but, lor'! you may just as well speak to a post as to Mr. Dunbar. If Miss Laura comes out in the park now, she must wrap herself up warm, and walk fast, and not go getting the cold shivers for the sake of drawing a parcel of stumps of trees and such-like tom-foolery."

Mrs. Madden made this observation in rather an unpleasant tone of voice one morning when the baronet pleaded for another drawing-lesson. The truth of the matter was that Elizabeth Madden felt some slight pangs of conscience with regard to her own part in this sudden friendship which had arisen between Laura Dunbar and Philip Jocelyn. She felt that she had been rather remiss in her duties as duenna, and was angry with herself. But stronger than this feeling of self-reproach was her indignation against Sir Philip.

Why did he not immediately make an offer of his hand to Laura Dunbar?

Mrs. Madden had expected the young man's proposal every day for the last few weeks: every day she had been doomed to disappointment. And yet she was perfectly convinced that Philip

Jocelyn loved her young mistress. The sharp eyes of the matron had fathomed the young man's sentiments long before Laura Dunbar dared to whisper to herself that she was beloved. Why, then, did he not propose? Who could be a more fitting bride for the lord of Jocelyn's Rock than queenly Laura Dunbar, with her splendid dower of wealth and beauty?

Full of these ambitious hopes, Elizabeth Madden had played her part of duenna with such discretion as to give the young people plenty of opportunity for sweet, half-whispered converse, for murmured confidences, soft and low as the cooing of turtle-doves. But in all these conversations no word hinting at an offer of marriage had dropped from the lips of Philip Jocelyn.

He was so happy with Laura; so happy in those pleasant meetings under the Maudesley elms, that no thought of any thing so commonplace as a stereotyped proposal of marriage had a place in his mind.

Did he love her? Of course he did: more dearly than he had ever before loved any human creature; except that tender and gentle being, whose image, vaguely beautiful, was so intermingled with the dreams and realities of his childhood in that dim period in which it is difficult to distinguish the shadows of the night from the events of the day,—that pale and lovely creature whom he had but just learned to call "mother," when she faded out of his life for ever.

It was only when the weather grew too cold for out-of-door drawing-lessons that Sir Philip began to think that it was time to contemplate the very serious business of a proposal. He would have to speak to the banker, and all that sort of thing, of course, the baronet thought, as he sat by the fire in the oak-panelled breakfast-room at the Rock, pulling his thick moustaches reflectively, and staring at the red embers on the open hearth. The young man idolized Laura; but he did *not* particularly affect the society of Henry Dunbar. The millionaire was very courteous, very conciliating: but there was something in his stiff politeness, his studied smile, his deliberate speech, something entirely vague and indefinable, which had the same chilly effect upon Sir Philip's friendliness, as a cold cellar has on delicate-flavoured port. The subtle aroma vanished under that dismal influence.

"He's *her* father, and I'd kneel down, like the little boys in the streets, and clean his boots, if he wanted them cleaned, because he *is* her father," thought the young man; "and yet, somehow or other, I can't get on with him."

No! between the Anglo-Indian banker and Sir Philip Jocelyn there was no sympathy. They had no tastes in common: or let me rather say, Henry Dunbar revealed no taste in common with those of the young man whose highest hope in life was to be his son-in-law. The frank-hearted young country gentleman tried in vain to conciliate him, or to advance from the cold outwork of ceremonious acquaintanceship into the inner stronghold of friendly intercourse.

But when Sir Philip, after much hesitation and deliberation, presented himself one morning in the banker's tapestried sitting-room, and unburdened his heart to that gentleman—stopping every now and then to stare at the maker's name imprinted upon the lining of his hat, as if that name had been a magical symbol whence he drew certain auguries by which he governed his speech —Mr. Dunbar was especially gracious. "Would he honour Sir Philip by intrusting his daughter's happiness to his keeping? would he bestow upon Sir Philip the inestimable blessing of that dear hand? Why of course he would, provided always that Laura wished it. In such a matter as this Laura's decision should be supreme. He never had contemplated interfering in his daughter's bestowal of her affections: so long as they were not wasted upon an unworthy object. He wished her to marry whom she pleased; provided that she married an honest man."

Mr. Dunbar gave a weary kind of sigh as he said this; but the sigh was habitual to him, and he apologised for and explained it sometimes by a reference to his liver, which was disordered by five-and-thirty years in an Indian climate.

"I wish Laura to marry," he said; "I shall

be glad when she has secured the protection of a good husband."

Sir Philip Jocelyn sprang up with his face all a-glow with rapture, and would fain have seized the banker's hand in token of his gratitude; but Henry Dunbar waved him off with an authoritative gesture.

"Good morning, Sir Philip," he said; "I am very poor company, and I shall be glad to be alone with the *Times*. You young men don't appreciate the *Times*. You want your newspapers filled with prize-fighting and boat-racing, and the last gossip from 'the Corner.' You'll find Miss Dunbar in the blue drawing-room. Speak to her as soon as you please; and let me know the result of the interview."

It is not often that the heiress of a million or thereabouts is quite so readily disposed of. Sir Philip Jocelyn walked on air as he quitted the banker's apartments.

"Who ever would have thought that he was such a delicious old brick?" he thought. "I expected any quantity of cold water; and instead of that, he sends me straight to my darling with *carte blanche* to go in and win, if I can. If I can! Suppose Laura doesn't love me, after all. Suppose she's only a beautiful coquette, who likes to see men go mad for love of her. And yet I won't think that; I won't be downhearted; I won't believe she's any thing but what she seems—an angel of purity and truth."

But, in spite of his belief in Laura's truth, the baronet's courage was very low when he went into the blue drawing-room, and found Miss Dunbar seated in a deep embayed window, with the sunshine lighting up her hair and gleaming amongst the folds of her violet silk dress. She had been drawing; but her sketching apparatus lay idle on the little table by her side, and one listless hand hung down upon her dress, with a pencil held loosely between the slender fingers. She was looking straight before her, out upon the sunlit lawn, all gorgeous with flaunting autumn flowers; and there was something dreamy, not to say pensive, in the attitude of her drooping head.

But she started presently at the sound of that manly footstep; the pencil dropped from between her idle fingers, and she rose and turned towards the intruder. The beautiful face was in shadow as she turned away from the window; but no shadow could hide its sudden brightness, the happy radiance which lit up that candid countenance, as Miss Dunbar recognised her visitor.

The lover thought that one look more precious than Jocelyn's Rock, and a baronetcy that dated from the days of England's first Stuarts,—that one glorious smile, which melted away in a moment, and gave place to bright maidenly blushes, fresh and beautiful as the dewy heart of an old-fashioned cabbage-rose gathered at sunrise.

That one smile was enough. Philip Jocelyn was no coxcomb, but he knew all at once that he was beloved, and that very few words were needed. A great many were said, nevertheless; and I do not think two happier people ever sat side by side in the late autumn sunshine than those two, who lingered in the deep embayed window till the sun was low in the rosy western sky, and told Philip

Jocelyn that his visit to Maudesley Abbey had very much exceeded the limits of a morning call.

So Philip Jocelyn was accepted. Early the next morning he called again upon Mr. Dunbar, and begged that an early date might be chosen for the wedding. The banker assented willingly enough to the proposition.

"Let the marriage take place in the first week in November," he said. "I am tired of living at Maudesley, and I want to get away to the Continent. Of course I must remain here to be present at my daughter's wedding."

Philip Jocelyn was only too glad to receive this permission to hurry the date of the ceremonial. He went at once to Laura, and told her what Mr. Dunbar had said. Mrs. Madden was indignant at this unceremonious manner of arranging matters.

"Where's my young lady's *trussaw* to be got at a moment's notice, I should like to know? A deal you gentlemen know about such things. It's no use talking, my lord, there ain't a dressmaker livin' as would undertake the wedding-clothes for a baronet's lady in little better than a month."

But Mrs. Madden's objections were speedily overruled. To tell the truth, the honest-hearted creature was very much pleased to find that her young lady was going to be a baronet's wife, after all. She forgot all about her old favourite, Arthur Lovell; and set herself to work to expedite that most important matter of the wedding-garments. A man came down express from Howell and James's to Maudesley Abbey, with a bundle of patterns; and silks and velvets, gauzes and laces, and almost every costly fabric that was made, were ordered for Miss Dunbar's equipment. West-end dressmakers were communicated with. A French milliner, who looked like a lady of fashion, arrived one morning at Maudesley Abbey, and for a couple of hours poor Laura had to endure the slow agony of "trying on;" while Mrs. Madden and Dora Macmahon discussed all the colours in the rainbow, and a great many new shades and combinations of colour, invented by aspiring French chemists.

CHAPTER IV.

A NEW LIFE.

FOR the first time in her life, Margaret Wilmot knew what it was to have friends, real and earnest friends, who interested themselves in her welfare, and were bent upon securing her happiness; and I must admit that in this particular case there was something more than friendship—something holier and higher in its character—the pure and unselfish love of an honourable man.

Clement Austin, the cashier at Dunbar, Dunbar, and Balderby's Anglo-Indian banking-house, had fallen in love with the modest hazel-eyed music-mistress, and had set himself to work to watch her, and to find out all about her, long before he was conscious of the real nature of his feelings.

He had begun by pitying her. He had pitied her because of her hard life, her loneliness, her beauty, which doubtless exposed her to many dangers that would have been spared to a plain woman.

Now, when a man allows himself to pity a very pretty girl, he places himself on a moral tight-rope; and he must be a moral Blondin if he expects to walk with any safety upon the narrow line which alone divides him from the great abyss called love.

There are not many Blondins either physical or intellectual; and the consequence is, that nine out of ten of the gentlemen who place themselves in this perilous position find the narrow line very slippery, and, before they have gone twenty paces, plunge overboard plump to the very bottom of the abyss, and are over head and ears in love before they know where they are.

Clement Austin fell in love with Margaret Wilmot; and his tender regard, his respectful devotion, were very new and sweet to the lonely girl. It would have been strange, then, under such circumstances, if his love had been hopeless.

He was in no very great hurry to declare himself; for he had a powerful ally in his mother, who adored her son, and would have allowed him to bring home a young negress, or a North-American squaw, to the maternal hearth, if such a bride had been necessary to his happiness.

Mrs. Austin very speedily discovered her son's secret; for he had taken little pains to conceal his feelings from the indulgent mother who had been his confidante ever since his first boyish loves at a Clapham seminary, within whose sacred walls he had been admitted on Tuesdays and Fridays to learn dancing in the delightful society of five-and-thirty young ladies.

Mrs. Austin confessed that she would rather her son had chosen some damsel who could lay claim to greater worldly advantages than those possessed by the young music-mistress; but when Clement looked disappointed, the good soul's heart melted all in a moment, and she declared, that if Margaret was only as good as she was pretty, and truly attached to her dear noble-hearted boy, she (Mrs. Austin) would ask no more.

It happened fortunately that she knew nothing

of Joseph Wilmot's antecedents, or of the letter addressed to Norfolk Island; or perhaps she might have made very strong objections to a match between her son and a young lady whose father had spent a considerable part of his life in a penal settlement.

"We will tell my mother nothing of the past, Miss Wilmot," Clement Austin said, "except that which concerns yourself alone. Let the history of your unhappy father's life remain a secret between you and me. My mother is very fond of you; I should be sorry, therefore, if she heard any thing to shock her prejudices. I wish her to love you better every day."

Clement Austin had his wish; for the kind-hearted widow grew every day more and more attached to Margaret Wilmot. She discovered that the girl had more than an ordinary talent for music; and she proposed that Margaret should take a prettily furnished first-floor in a pleasant-looking detached house, half cottage, half villa, at Clapham, and at once set to work as a teacher of the piano.

"I can get you plenty of pupils, my dear," Mrs. Austin said; "for I have lived here more than thirty years—ever since Clement's birth, in fact—and I know almost every body in the neighbourhood. You have only to teach upon moderate terms, and the people will be glad to send their children to you. I shall give a little evening party, on purpose that my friends may hear you play."

So Mrs. Austin gave her evening party, and Margaret appeared in a simple black-silk dress that had been in her wardrobe for a long time, and which would have seemed very shabby in the glaring light of day. The wearer of it looked very pretty and elegant, however, by the light of Mrs. Austin's wax-candles; and the aristocracy of Clapham remarked that the "young person" whom Mrs. Austin and her son had "taken up" was really rather nice-looking.

But when Margaret played and sang, people were charmed in spite of themselves. She had a superb contralto voice, rich, deep, and melodious; and she played with brilliancy, and what is much rarer, with expression.

Mrs. Austin, going backwards and forwards amongst her guests to ascertain the current of opinions, found that her protégée's success was an accomplished fact before the evening was over.

Margaret took the new apartments in the course of the week; and before a fortnight had passed, she had secured more than a dozen pupils, who gave her ample employment for her time; and who enabled her to earn more than enough for her simple wants.

Every Sunday she dined with Mrs. Austin. Clement had persuaded his mother to make this arrangement a settled thing; although as yet he had said nothing of his growing love for Margaret.

Those Sundays were pleasant days to Clement and the girl whom he hoped to win for his wife.

The comfortable elegance of Mrs. Austin's drawing-room, the peaceful quiet of the Sabbath-evening, when the curtains were drawn before the bay-window, and the shaded lamp brought into the room; the intellectual conversation; the pleasant talk about new books and music: all were new and delightful to Margaret.

This was her first experience of a home, a real home, in which there was nothing but union and content; no overshadowing fear, no horrible unspoken dread, no half-guessed secrets always gnawing at the heart. But in all this new comfort Margaret Wilmot had not forgotten Henry Dunbar. She had not ceased to believe him guilty of her father's murder. Calm and gentle in her outward demeanour, she kept her secret buried in her breast, and asked for no sympathy.

Clement Austin had given her his best attention, his best advice; but it all amounted to nothing. The different scraps of evidence that hinted at Henry Dunbar's guilt were not strong enough to condemn him. The cashier communicated with the detective police, who had been watching the case; but they only shook their heads gravely, and dismissed him with their thanks for his information. There was nothing in what he had to tell them that could implicate Mr. Dunbar.

"A gentleman with a million of money doesn't put himself in the power of the hangman unless he's very hard pushed," said the detective. "The motive 's what you must look to in these cases, sir. Now, where's Mr. Dunbar's motive for murdering this man Wilmot?"

"The secret that Joseph Wilmot possessed——"

"Bah, my dear sir! Henry Dunbar could afford to buy all the secrets that ever were kept. Secrets are like every other sort of article: they're only kept to sell. Good morning."

After this, Clement Austin told Margaret that he could be of no use to her. The dead man must rest in his grave: there was little hope that the mystery of his fate would ever be fathomed by human intelligence.

But Margaret Wilmot did not cease to remember Mr. Dunbar. She only waited.

One resolution was always uppermost in her mind, even when she was happiest with her new friends. She would see Henry Dunbar. In spite of his obstinate determination to avoid an interview with her, she would see him: and then, when she had gained her purpose, and stood face to face with him, she would boldly denounce him as her father's murderer. If then he did not flinch or falter, if she saw innocence in his face, she would cease to doubt him, she would be content to believe that Joseph Wilmot had met his untimely death from a stranger's hand.

CHAPTER V.

THE STEEPLE-CHASE.

AFTER considerable discussion, it was settled that Laura Dunbar's wedding should take place upon the 7th of November. It was to be a very quiet wedding. The banker had especially impressed that condition upon his daughter. His health was entirely broken, and he would assist in no splendid ceremonial to which half the county would be invited. If Laura wanted bridesmaids, she might have Dora Macmahon and any particular friend who lived in the neighbourhood. There was to be no fuss, no publicity. Marriage was a very solemn business, Mr. Dunbar said, and it would be as well for his daughter to be undisturbed by any pomp or gaiety on her wedding-day. So the marriage was appointed to take place on the 7th, and the arrangements were to be as simple as the circumstances of the bride would admit. Sir Philip was quite willing that it should be so. He was much too happy to take objection to any such small matters. He only wanted the sacred words to be spoken which made Laura Dunbar his own for ever and for ever. He wanted to take her away to the southern regions, where he had travelled so gaily in his careless bachelor days, where he would be so supremely happy now with his bright young bride by his side. Fortune, who certainly spoils some of her children, had been especially beneficent to this young man. She had given him so many of her best gifts, and had bestowed upon him, over and above, the power to enjoy her favours.

It happened that the 6th of November was a day which, some time since, Philip Jocelyn would have considered the most important, if not the happiest day of the year. It was the date of the Shorncliffe steeple-chases, and the baronet had engaged himself early in the preceding spring to ride his thoroughbred mare Guinevere, for a certain silver cup, subscribed for by the officers stationed at the Shorncliffe barracks.

Philip Jocelyn looked forward to this race with a peculiar interest, for it was to be the last he would ever ride—the very last; he had given this solemn promise to Laura, who had in vain tried to persuade him against even this race. She was brave enough upon ordinary occasions; but she loved her betrothed husband too dearly to be brave on this.

"I know it's very foolish of me, Philip," she said, "but I can't help being frightened. I can't help thinking of all the accidents I've ever heard of, or read of. I've dreamt of the race ever so many times, Philip. Oh, if you would only give it up for my sake!"

"My darling, my pet, is there any thing I would *not* do for your sake that I could do in honour? But I can't do this, Laura dearest. You see I'm all right myself, and the mare's in splendid condition;—well, you saw her take her trial gallop the other morning, and you must know she's a flyer, so I won't talk about her. My name was entered for this race six months ago, you know, dear; and there are lots of small farmers and country people who have speculated their money on me; and they'd all lose, poor fellows, if I hung back at the last. You don't know what play-or-pay bets are, Laura dear. There's nothing in the world I wouldn't do for your sake; but my backers are poor people, and I can't put them in a hole. I must ride, Laura, and ride to win too."

Miss Dunbar knew what this last phrase meant, and she conjured up the image of her lover flying across country on that fiery chestnut mare, whose reputation was familiar to almost every man, woman, and child in Warwickshire: but whatever her fears might be, she was obliged to be satisfied with her lover's promise that this should be his last steeple-chase.

The day came at last, a pale November day, mild but not sunny. The sky was all of one equal gray tint, and seemed to hang only a little way above the earth. The caps and jackets of the gentleman riders made spots of colour against that uniform gray sky; and the dresses of the ladies in the humble wooden structure which did duty as a grand stand, brightened the level landscape.

The course formed a long oval, and extended over three or four meadows, and crossed a country lane. It was a tolerably flat course; but the leaps, though roughly constructed, were rather formidable. Laura had been over all the ground with her lover on the previous day, and had looked fearfully at the high ragged hedges, and the broad ditches of muddy water. But Philip only made light of her fears, and told her the leaps were nothing, scarcely worthy of the chestnut mare's powers.

The course was not crowded, but there was a considerable sprinkling of spectators on each side of the ropes—soldiers from the Shorncliffe barracks, country people, and loiterers of all kinds. There were a couple of drags, crowded with the officers and their friends, who clustered in all manner of perilous positions on the roof, and consumed unlimited champagne, bitter beer, and lobster-salad, in the pauses between the races. A single line of carriages extended for some little distance opposite the grand stand. The scene was gay and pleasant, as a race-ground always must be, even though it were in the wildest regions of the New World; but it was very quiet as compared to Epsom Downs or the open heath at Ascot.

Conspicuous amongst the vehicles there was a close carriage drawn by a pair of magnificent bays —an equipage which was only splendid in the perfection of its appointments. It was a clarence, with dark subdued-looking panels, only ornamented by a vermilion crest. The liveries of the servants were almost the simplest upon the course; but the powdered heads of the men, and an indescribable something in their style, distinguished them from the country-bred coachmen and hobbledehoy pages in attendance on the other carriages.

Almost every one on the course knew that crest of an armed hand clasping a battleaxe, and knew that it belonged to Henry Dunbar. The banker appeared so very seldom in public that there was always a kind of curiosity about him when he did show himself; and between the races, people who were strolling upon the ground contrived to approach very near the carriage in which the master of Maudesley Abbey sat, wrapped in Cashmere shawls, and half-hidden under a great fur rug, in legitimate Indian fashion.

He had consented to appear upon the race-course in compliance with his daughter's most urgent entreaties. She wanted him to be near her. She had some vague idea that he might be useful in the event of any accident happening to Philip Jocelyn. He might help her. It would be some consolation, some support to have him with her. He might be able to do something. Her father had yielded to her entreaties with a very tolerable grace, and he was here; but having conceded so much, he seemed to have done all that his frigid nature was capable of doing. He took no interest in the business of the day, but lounged far back in the carriage, and complained very much of the cold.

The vehicle had been drawn close up to the boundary of the course, and Laura sat at the open window, pale and anxious, straining her eyes towards the weighing-house, and the paddock, the little bit of enclosed ground where the horses were saddled. She could see the gentleman riders going in and out, and the one rider on whose safety her happiness depended, muffled in his greatcoat, and very busy and animated amongst his grooms and helpers. Every body knew who Miss Dunbar was, and that she was going to be married to the young baronet; and people looked with interest at that pale face keeping such anxious watch at the carriage-window. I am speaking now of the simple country people, for whom a race meant a day's pleasure. There were people on the other side of the course who cared very little for Miss Dunbar or her anxiety; who would have cared as little if the handsome young baronet had rolled upon the sward, crushed to death under the weight of his chestnut mare, so long as they themselves were winners by the event. In the little enclosure below the grand stand, the betting men—that strange fraternity which appears on every race-course from Berwick-on-Tweed to the Land's-End, from the banks of the Shannon to the smooth meads of pleasant Normandy—were gathered thick, and the talk was loud about Sir Philip and his competitors.

Among the men who were ready to lay against

any thing, and were most unpleasantly vociferous in the declaration of their readiness, there was one man who was well known to the humbler class of bookmen with whom he associated, who was known to speculate upon very small capital, but who had never been known as a defaulter. The knowing ones declared this man worthy to rank high amongst the best of them; but no one knew where he lived, or what he was. He was rarely known to miss a race; and he was conspicuous amongst the crowd in those mysterious purlieus where the plebeian bookmen, who are unworthy to enter the sacred precincts of Tattersall's, mostly do congregate, in utter defiance of the police. No one had ever heard the name of this man; but in default of any more particular cognomen, they had christened him the Major; because in his curt manners, his closely buttoned-up coat, tightly-strapped trousers, and heavy moustache, there was a certain military flavour, which had given rise to the rumour, that the unknown had in some remote period been one of the defenders of his country. Whether he had enlisted as a private, and had been bought off by his friends; whether he had borne the rank of an officer, and had sold his commission, or had been cashiered, or had deserted, or had been drummed out of his regiment,—no one pretended to say. People called him the Major; and wherever he appeared, the Major made himself conspicuous by means of a very tall white hat with a broad black crape band round it.

He was tall himself, and the hat made him seem taller. His clothes were very shabby, with that peculiar shiny shabbiness which makes a man look as if he had been oiled all over, and then rubbed into a high state of polish. He wore a greenish-brown greatcoat with a poodle collar, and was supposed to have worn the same for the last ten years. Round his neck, be the weather ever so sultry, he wore a comforter of rusty worsted that had once been scarlet, and above this comforter appeared his nose, which was a prominent aquiline. Nobody ever saw much more of the Major than his nose and his moustache. His hat came low down over his forehead, which was itself low, and a pair of beetle brows, of a dense purple-black, were faintly visible in the shadow of the brim. He never took off his hat in the presence of his fellow-men; and as he never encountered the fair sex, except in the person of the barmaid at a sporting public, he was not called upon to unbonnet himself in ceremonious obeisance to lovely woman. He was eminently a mysterious man, and seemed to enjoy himself in the midst of the cloud of mystery which surrounded him.

The Major had inspected the starters for the great event of the day, and had sharply scrutinised the gentleman riders as they went in and out of the paddock. He was so well satisfied with the look of Sir Philip Jocelyn, and the chestnut mare Guinevere, that he contented himself with laying the odds against all the other horses, and allowed the baronet and the chestnut to run for him. He asked a few questions presently about Sir Philip, who had taken off his greatcoat by this time, and appeared in all the glory of a scarlet satin jacket and a black velvet cap. A Warwickshire farmer, who had found his way in among the knowing ones, informed the Major that Sir Philip

Jocelyn was going to be married to Miss Dunbar, only daughter and sole heiress of the great Mr. Dunbar.

The great Mr. Dunbar! The Major, usually so imperturbable, gave a little start at the mention of the banker's name.

"What Mr. Dunbar?" he asked.

"The banker. Him as come home from the Indies last August."

The Major gave a long low whistle; but he asked no further question of the farmer. He had a memorandum-book in his hand—a greasy and grimy-looking little volume, whose pages he was wont to study profoundly from time to time, and in which he jotted down all manner of queer hieroglyphics with half an inch of fat lead-pencil. He relapsed into the contemplation of this book now; but he muttered to himself ever and anon in undertones, and his mutterings had relation to Henry Dunbar.

"It's him," he muttered; "that's lucky. I read all about that Winchester business in the Sunday papers. I've got it all at my fingers'-

ends, and I don't see why I shouldn't make a trifle out of it. I don't see why I shouldn't win a little money upon Henry Dunbar. I'll have a look at my gentleman presently, when the race is over."

The bell rang, and the seven starters went off with a rush; four abreast, and three behind. Sir Philip was among the four foremost riders, keeping the chestnut well in hand, and biding his time very quietly. This was his last race, and he had set his heart upon winning. Laura leaned out of the carriage-window, pale and breathless, with a powerful race-glass in her hand. She watched the riders as they swept round the curve in the course. Then they disappeared, and the few minutes during which they were out of sight seemed an age to that anxious watcher. The people run away to see them take the double leap in the lane, and then come trooping back again, panting and eager, as three of the riders appear again round another bend of the course.

The scarlet leads this time. The honest country people hurrah for the master of Jocelyn's Rock.

Have they not put their money upon him, and are they not proud of him?—proud of his handsome face, which, amid all its easy goodnature, has a certain dash of hauteur that befits one who has a sprinkling of the blood of Saxon kings in his veins; proud of his generous heart, which beats with a thousand kindly impulses towards his fellow-men. They shout aloud as he flies past them, the long stride of the chestnut skimming over the ground, and spattering fragments of torn grass and ploughed-up earth about him as he goes. Laura sees the scarlet jacket rise for a moment against the low gray sky, and then fly onward, and that is about all she sees of the dreaded leap which she had looked at in fear and trembling the day before. Her heart is still beating with a strange vague terror, when her lover rides quietly past the stand, and the people about her cry out that the race has been nobly won. The other riders come in very slowly, and are oppressed by that indescribable air of sheepishness which is peculiar to gentleman jockeys when they do not win.

The girl's eyes fill suddenly with tears, and she leans back in the carriage, glad to hide her happy face from the crowd.

Ten minutes afterwards Sir Philip Jocelyn came across the course with a great silver-gilt cup in his arms, and surrounded by an admiring throng, amongst whom he had just emptied his purse.

"I've brought you the cup, Laura; and I want you to be pleased with my victory. It's the last triumph of my bachelor days, you know, darling."

"Three cheers for Miss Dunbar!" shouted some adventurous spirit among the crowd about the baronet.

In the next moment the cry was taken up, and two or three hundred voices joined in a loud hurrah for the banker's daughter. The poor girl drew back into the carriage blushing and frightened.

"Don't mind them, Laura dear," Sir Philip said; "they mean well, you know, and they look upon me as public property. Hadn't you better give them a bow, Mr. Dunbar?" he added in an undertone to the banker. "It'll please them, I know."

Mr. Dunbar frowned, but he bent forward for a moment, and, leaning his head a little way out of the window, made a stately acknowledgment of the people's enthusiasm. As he did so, his eyes met those of the Major, who had crossed the course with Sir Philip and his admirers, and who was staring straight before him at the banker's carriage. Henry Dunbar drew back immediately after making that very brief salute to the populace.

"Tell them to drive home, Sir Philip," he said. "The people mean well, I daresay; but I hate these popular demonstrations. There's something to be done about the settlements, by the by; you'd better dine at the Abbey this evening. John Lovell will be there to meet you."

The carriage drove away; and though the Major pushed his way through the crowd pretty rapidly, he was too late to witness its departure.

He was in a very good temper, however; for he had won what his companions called a hatful of money on the steeple-chase, and he stood to win on other races that were to come off that afternoon. During the interval that elapsed before the next race, he talked to a sociable bystander about Sir Philip Jocelyn, and the young lady he was going to marry. He ascertained that the wedding was to take place the next morning, and at Lisford church.

"In that case," thought the Major, as he went back to the ring, "I shall sleep at Lisford to-night; I shall make Lisford my quarters for the present; and I shall follow up Henry Dunbar."

CHAPTER VI.

THE BRIDE THAT THE RAIN RAINS ON.

THERE was no sunshine upon Laura Dunbar's wedding morning. The wintry sky was low and dark; as if the heavens had been coming gradually down to crush this wicked earth. The damp fog, the slow, drizzling rain, shut out the fair landscape upon which the banker's daughter had been wont to look from the pleasant cushioned seat in the deep bay-window of her dressing-room.

The broad lawn was soddened by that perpetual rain. The incessant rain-drops dripped from the low branches of the black spreading cedars of Lebanon; the smooth beads of water ran off the shining laurel-leaves; the rhododendrons, the feathery furze, the glistening arbutus—every thing was obscured by that cruel rain.

The water gushed out of the quaint dragons'

mouths ranged along the parapet of the Abbey roof; it dripped from every stone coping and abutment; from window-ledge and porch, from gabel-end and sheltering ivy. The rain was everywhere; and the incessant pitter-patter of the drops beating against the windows of the Abbey made a dismal sound, scarcely less unpleasant to hear than the perpetual lamentation of the winds, which to-day had the sound of human voices; now moaning drearily, with a long, low, wailing murmur, now shrieking in the shrilly tones of an angry vixen.

Laura Dunbar gave a long discontented sigh as she seated herself at her favourite bay-window and looked out at the dripping trees upon the lawn below.

She was a petted heiress, remember, and the world had gone so smoothly with her hitherto, that perhaps she scarcely endured calamity or contradiction with so good a grace as she might have done, had she been a little nearer perfection. She was hardly better than a child as yet, with all a child's ignorant hopefulness and blind trust in the unknown future. She was a pampered child; and she expected to have life made very smooth for her.

"What a horribly dismal morning!" Miss Dunbar exclaimed. "Did you ever see any thing like it, Elizabeth?"

Mrs. Madden was bustling about, arranging her young mistress's breakfast upon a little table near the blazing fire. Laura had just emerged from her bath-room, and had put on a loose dressing-gown of wadded blue silk, prior to the grand ceremonial of the wedding toilet, which was not to take place until after breakfast.

I think Miss Dunbar looked lovelier in this *déshabille* than many a bride in her lace and orange-blossoms. The girl's long golden hair, wet from the bath, hung in rippling confusion about her fresh young face. Two little feet, carelessly thrust into blue morocco slippers, peeped out from amongst the folds of Miss Dunbar's dressing-gown, and one coquettish scarlet heel tapped impatiently upon the floor as the young lady watched that provoking rain.

"What a wretched morning!" she said.

"Well, Miss Laura, it is rather wet," replied Mrs. Madden, in a conciliating tone.

"Rather wet!" echoed Laura, with an air of vexation; "I should think it was *rather* wet, indeed. It's miserably wet; it's horribly wet. To think that the frost should have lasted very nearly three weeks; and then must needs break up on my wedding morning. Did ever any body know any thing so provoking?"

"Lor', Miss Laura," rejoined the sympathetic Madden, "there's all manner of provoking things allus happenin' in this blessed, wicked, rampagious world of ours; only such young ladies as you don't often come across 'em. Talk of being born with a silver spoon in your mouth, Miss Laura; I do think as you must have come into this mortal spear with a whole service of gold plate. And don't you fret your precious heart, my blessed Miss Laura, if the rain *is* contrairy. I daresay the clerk of the weather is one of them rampagin' radicals that's allus a goin' on about the bloated aristocracy, and he's done it a purpose to aggeravate you. But what's a little rain more or less to you, Miss Laura, when you've got more carriages to ride in than if you was a princess in a fairy tale, which I think the Princess Baltroubadore, or whatever her hard name was, in the story of Aladdin, must have had no carriage whatever, or she wouldn't have gone walkin' to the baths. Never you mind the rain, Miss Laura."

"But it's a bad omen, isn't it, Elizabeth?" asked Laura Dunbar. "I seem to remember some old rhyme about the bride that the sun shines on, and the bride that the rain rains on."

"Laws, Miss Laura, you don't mean to say as you'd bemean yourself by taking any heed of such low rubbish as that!" exclaimed Mrs. Madden; "why such stupid rhymes as them are only made for vulgar people that have the banns put up in the parish-church. A deal it matters to such as you, Miss Laura, if all the cats and dogs as ever was come down out of the heavens this blessed day."

But though honest-hearted Elizabeth Madden did her best to comfort her young mistress after her own simple fashion, she was not herself altogether satisfied.

The low, brooding sky, the dark and murky atmosphere, and that monotonous rain, would have gone far to depress the spirits of the gayest reveller in all the universe.

In spite of ourselves, we are the slaves of atmospheric influences; and we cannot feel very light-hearted or happy upon black wintry days; when the lowering heavens seem to frown upon our hopes; when, in the darkening of the earthly prospect, we fancy that we see a shadowy curtain closing round an unknown future.

Laura felt something of this; for she said, by and by, half impatiently, half mournfully—

"What *is* the matter with me, Elizabeth? Has all the world changed since yesterday? When I drove home with papa, after the races yesterday, every thing upon earth seemed so bright and beautiful. Such an overpowering sense of joy was in my heart, that I could scarcely believe it was winter, and that it was only the fading November sunshine that lit up the sky. All my future life seemed spread before me, like an endless series of beautiful pictures—pictures in which I could see Philip and myself, always together, always happy. To-day, to-day, oh! *how* different every thing is!" exclaimed Laura, with a little shudder. "The sky that shuts in the lawn yonder seems to shut in my life with it. I can't look forward. If I was going to be parted from Philip to-day, instead of married to him, I don't think I could feel more miserable than I feel now. Why is it, Elizabeth dear?"

"My goodness gracious me!" cried Mrs. Madden, "how should I tell, my precious pet? You talk just like a poetry-book, and how can I answer you unless I was another poetry-book? Come and have your breakfast, do, that's a dear sweet love, and try a new-laid egg. New-laid eggs is good for the spirits, my poppet."

Laura Dunbar seated herself in the comfortable arm-chair between the fireplace and the little breakfast-table. She made a sort of pretence of eating, just to please her old nurse, who fidgeted about the room; now stopping by Laura's chair, and urging her to take this, that, or the other; now running to the dressing-table to make some new arrangement about the all-important wedding toilet; now looking out of the window and perjuring her simple soul by declaring that "it"—namely, the winter sky—was going to clear up.

"It's breaking up above the elms yonder, Miss Laura," Elizabeth said; "there's a bit of blue peepin' through the clouds; leastways, if it ain't quite blue, it's a much lighter black than the rest of the sky, and that's somethin'. Eat a bit of Perrigorge pie, or a thin wafer of a slice off that Strasbog 'am, Miss Laura, do now. You'll be ready to drop with feelin' faint when you get to the altar-rails, if you persist on bein' married on a empty stummick, Miss Laura. It's a moriel impossible as you can look your best, my precious love, if you enter the church in a state of starvation, just like one of them respectable beggars wot pins a piece of paper on their weskits with 'I AM HUNGRY' wrote upon it in large-hand, and stands at the foot of one of the bridges on the Surrey side of the water. And I shouldn't think as you would wish to look like *that*, Miss Laura, on your wedding-day? *I* shouldn't, if *I* was goin' to be own wife to a baronet!"

Laura Dunbar took very little notice of her nurse's rambling discourse; and I am fain to confess that, upon this occasion, Mrs. Madden talked rather more for the sake of talking, than from any overflow of animal spirits.

The good creature felt the influence of the cold, wet, cheerless morning quite as keenly as her mistress. Mrs. Madden was superstitious, as most ignorant and simple-minded people generally are, more or less. Superstition is, after all, only a dim, unconscious poetry, which is latent in most natures, except in such very hard practical minds as are incapable of believing in any thing—not even in Heaven itself.

Dora Macmahon came in presently, looking very pretty in blue silk and white lace. She looked very happy, in spite of the bad weather, and Miss Dunbar suffered herself to be comforted by her half-sister. The two girls sat at the table by the fire, and breakfasted, or pretended to breakfast together. Who could really attend to the common business of eating and drinking on such a day as this?

"I've just been to see Lizzie and Ellen," Dora said, presently; "they wouldn't come in here till they were dressed, and they've had their hair screwed up in hair-pins all night to make it wave, and now it's a wet day their hair won't wave after all, and their maid's going to pinch it with the fire-irons—the tongs, I suppose."

Miss Macmahon had brown hair with a natural ripple in it, and could afford to laugh at beauty that was obliged to adorn itself by means of hair-pins and tongs.

Lizzie and Ellen were the daughters of a Major Melville, and the special friends of Miss Dunbar. They had come to Maudesley to act as her bridesmaids, according to that favourite promise which young ladies so often make to each other, and so very often break.

Laura did not appear to take much interest in the Miss Melvilles' hair. She was very meditative about something; but her meditations must have been of a pleasant nature, for there was a smile upon her face.

"Dora," she said, by and by, "do you know I've been thinking about something?"

"About what, dear?"

"Don't you know that old saying about one wedding making many?"

Dora Macmahon blushed.

"What of that, Laura dear?" she asked, very innocently.

"I've been thinking that perhaps another wedding may follow mine. Oh, Dora, I can't help saying it, I should be so happy if Arthur Lovell and you were to marry."

Miss Macmahon blushed a much deeper red than before.

"Oh, Laura," she said, "that's quite impossible."

But Miss Dunbar shook her head.

"I shall live in the hope of it, notwithstanding," she said. "I love Arthur almost as much—or perhaps quite as much, as if he were my brother—so it isn't strange that

I should wish to see him married to my sister."

The two girls might have sat talking for some time longer, but they were interrupted by Miss Dunbar's old nurse, who never for a moment lost sight of the serious business of the day.

"It's all very well for you to sit there jabber, jabber, jabber, Miss Dora," exclaimed the unceremonious Elizabeth; "you're dressed, all but your bonnet. You've only just to pop that on, and there you are. But my young lady isn't half dressed yet. And now, come along, Miss Laura, and have your hair done, if you mean to have any back-hair at all to-day. It's past nine o'clock, and you're to be at the church at eleven."

"And papa is to give me away!" murmured Laura, in a low voice, as she seated herself before the dressing-table. "I wish he loved me better."

"Perhaps, if he loved you too well, he'd keep you, instead of giving you away, Miss Laura," observed Mrs. Madden, with evident enjoyment of her own wit; "and I don't suppose you'd care about that, would you, miss? Hold your head still, that's a precious darling, and don't you trouble yourself about any thing except looking your very best this day."

CHAPTER VII.

THE UNBIDDEN GUEST WHO CAME TO LAURA DUNBAR'S WEDDING.

THE wedding was to take place in Lisford church—that pretty, quaint, old church of which I have already spoken.

The wandering Avon flowed through this rustic churchyard, along a winding channel fringed by tall, trembling rushes. There was a wooden bridge across the river, and there were two opposite entrances to the churchyard. Pedestrians who chose the shortest route between Lisford and Shorncliffe went in at one gate and out at another, which opened on to the high road.

The worthy inhabitants of Lisford were almost as much distressed by the unpromising aspect of the sky as Laura Dunbar and her faithful nurse themselves. New bonnets had been specially prepared for this festive occasion. Chrysanthemums and dahlias, gay-looking China asters, and all the lingering flowers that light up the early-winter landscape, had been collected to strew the pathway beneath the bride's pretty feet. All the brightest evergreens in the Lisford gardens had been gathered as a fitting sacrifice for the "young lady from the Abbey."

Laura Dunbar's frank good-nature and reckless generosity were well remembered upon this occasion; and every creature in Lisford was bent upon doing her honour.

But this aggravating rain baulked every body. What was the use of throwing wet dahlias and flabby chrysanthemums into the puddles through which the bride must tread, heiress though she was? How miserable would be the aspect of two rows of damp charity-children, with red noses and no pocket-handkerchiefs! The rector himself had a cold in his head, and would be obliged to omit all the *n*'s and *m*'s in the marriage service.

In short, every body felt that the Abbey wedding was destined to be more or less a failure. It seemed very hard that the chief partner in the firm of Dunbar, Dunbar, and Balderby could not, with all his wealth, buy a little glimmer of sunshine to light up his daughter's wedding. It grew so dark and foggy towards eleven o'clock, that a dozen or so of wax-candles were hastily stuck about the neighbourhood of the altar, in order that the bride and bridegroom might be able, each of them, to see the person that he or she was taking for better or worse.

Yes, the dismal weather made every thing dismal in unison with itself. A wet wedding is like a wet pic-nic. The most heroic nature gives way before its utter desolation; the wit of the party forgets his best anecdote; the funny man breaks down in the climakic verse of his great buffo song; there is no brightness in the eyes of the beauty; there is neither sparkle nor flavour in the champagne, though the grapes thereof have been grown in the vineyards of Widow Cliquot herself.

There are some things that are more powerful than emperors, and the atmosphere is one of them. Alexander might conquer nations in very sport;

but I question whether he could have resisted the influence of a wet day.

Of all the people who were to assist at Sir Philip Jocelyn's wedding, perhaps the father of the bride was the person who seemed least affected by that drizzling rain, that hopelessly-black sky.

If Henry Dunbar was grave and silent to-day, why that was nothing new: for he was always grave and silent. If the banker's manner was stern and moody to-day, that stern moodiness was habitual to him: and there was no need to blame the murky heavens for any change in his temper. He sat by the broad fireplace watching the burning coals, and waiting until he should be summoned to take his place by his daughter's side in the carriage that was to convey them both to Lisford church; and he did not utter one word of complaint about that aggravating weather.

He looked very handsome, very aristocratic, with his gray moustache carefully trimmed, and a white camellia in his button-hole. Nevertheless, when he came out into the hall by and by, with a set smile upon his face, like a man who is going to act a part in a play, Laura Dunbar recoiled from him with an involuntary shiver, as she had done upon the day of her first meeting with him in Portland Place.

But he offered her his hand, and she laid the tips of her fingers in his broad palm, and went with him to the carriage.

"Ask God to bless me upon this day, papa," the girl said, in a low, tender voice, as these two people took their places side by side in the roomy chariot.

Laura Dunbar laid her hand caressingly upon the banker's shoulder as she spoke. It was not a time for reticence: it was not an occasion upon which to be put off by any girlish fear of this stern, silent man.

"Ask God to bless me, father dearest," the soft, tremulous voice pleaded, "for the sake of my dead mother."

She tried to see his face: but she could not. His head was turned away, and he was busy making some alteration in the adjustment of the carriage-window. The chariot had cost nearly three hundred pounds, and was very well built: but there was something wrong about the window nevertheless, if one might judge by the difficulty which Mr. Dunbar had in settling it to his satisfaction.

He spoke presently, in a very earnest voice, but with his head still turned away from Laura.

"I hope God will bless you, my dear," he said; "and that He will have pity upon your enemies."

This last wish was more Christianlike than natural; since fathers do not usually implore compassion for the enemies of their children.

But Laura Dunbar did not trouble herself to think about this. She only knew that her father had called down Heaven's blessing upon her; and that his manner had betrayed such agitation as could, of course, only spring from one cause, namely, his affection for his daughter.

She threw herself into his arms with a radiant smile, and, putting up her hands, drew his face round, and pressed her lips to his.

But, as on the day in Portland Place, a chill

crept through her veins, as she felt the deadly coldness of her father's hands lifted to push her gently from him.

It is a common thing for Anglo-Indians to be quiet and reserved in their manners, and strongly adverse to all demonstrations of this kind. Laura remembered this, and made excuses to herself for her father's coldness.

The rain was still falling as the carriage stopped at the churchyard. There were only three carriages in this brief bridal train, for Mr. Dunbar had insisted that there should be no grandeur, no display.

The two Miss Melvilles, Dora Macmahon, and Arthur Lovell rode in the same carriage. Major Melville's daughters looked very pale and cold in their white-and-blue dresses, and the north-easter had tweaked their noses, which were rather sharp and pointed in style. They would have looked pretty enough, poor girls, had the wedding taken place in summer time; but they had not that splendid exceptional beauty which can defy all changes of temperature, and which is alike glorious, whether clad in abject rags or robed in velvet and ermine.

The carriages reached the little gate of Lisford churchyard; Philip Jocelyn came out of the porch, and down the narrow pathway leading to the gate.

The drizzling rain descended on him, though he was a baronet, and though he came bareheaded to receive his bride.

I think the Lisford beadle, who was a sound Tory of the old school, almost wondered that the heavens themselves should be audacious enough to wet the uncovered head of the lord of Jocelyn's Rock.

But it went on raining, nevertheless.

"Times has changed, sir," said the beadle, to an idle-looking stranger who was standing near him. "I have read in a history of Warwickshire, that when Algernon Jocelyn was married to Dame Margery Milward, widow to Sir Stephen Milward, Knight, in Charles the First's time, there was a cloth-of-gold canopy from the gate yonder to this porch here, and two moving turrets of basket-work, each of 'em drawn by four horses, and filled with forty poor children, crowned with roses, lookin' out of the turret winders, and scatterin' scented waters on the crowd; and there was a banquet, sir, served up at noon that day at Jocelyn's Rock, with six peacocks brought to table with their tails spread; and a pie, served in a gold dish, with live doves in it, every feather of 'em steeped in the rarest perfume, which they was intended to sprinkle over the company as they flew about here and there. But—would you believe in such a radical spirit pervadin' the animal creation?—every one of them doves flew straight out of the winder, and went and scattered their perfumes on the poor folks outside. There's no such weddin's as that nowadays, sir," said the old beadle, with a groan. "As I often say to my old missus, I don't believe as ever England has held up its head since the day when Charles the Martyr lost his'n."

Laura Dunbar went up the narrow pathway by her father's side; but Philip Jocelyn walked upon her left hand, and the crowd had enough to do to stare at bride and bridegroom.

The baronet's face, which was always a handsome one, looked splendid in the light of his happiness. People disputed as to whether the bride or bridegroom was handsomest; and Laura forgot all about the wet weather as she laid her light hand on Philip Jocelyn's arm.

The churchyard was densely crowded in the neighbourhood of the pathway along which the bride and bridegroom walked. In spite of the miserable weather, in defiance of Mr. Dunbar's desire that the wedding should be a quiet one, people had come from a very long distance, in order to see the millionaire's beautiful daughter married to the master of Jocelyn's Rock.

Amongst the spectators who had come to witness Miss Dunbar's wedding was the tall gentleman in the high white hat who was known in sporting circles as the Major, and who had exhibited so much interest when the name of Henry Dunbar was mentioned on the Shorncliffe race-course. The Major had been very lucky in his speculations on the Shorncliffe races, and had gone straight away from the course to the village of Lisford, where he took up his abode at the Rose and Crown,—a bright-looking hostelry, where a traveller could have his steak or his chop done to a turn in one of the cosiest kitchens in all Warwickshire. The Major was very reserved upon the subject of his sporting operations when he found himself among unprofessional people; and upon such occasions, though he would now and then condescend to lay the odds against any thing with some unconscious agriculturalist or village tradesman, his innocence with regard to all turf matters was positively refreshing.

He was a traveller in Birmingham jewelry, he told the landlady of the quiet little inn, and was on his way to that busy commercial centre, to procure a fresh supply of glass emeralds, and a score or so of gigantic rubies with crinkled tinsel behind them. The Major, usually somewhat silent and morose, contrived to make himself very agreeable to the jovial frequenters of the comfortable little public parlour of the Rose and Crown.

He took his dinner and his supper in that cosy apartment; and he sat there all the evening, listening to and joining in the conversation of the Lisfordians, and drinking sixpenn'orths of gin-and-water, with the air of a man who could consume a hogshead of the juice of the juniper-berry without experiencing any evil consequences therefrom. He ate and drank like a man of iron; and his glittering black eyes kept perpetual watch upon the faces of the simple country people, and his eager ears drank in every word that was spoken. Of course a great deal was said about the event of the next morning. Every body had something to say about Miss Dunbar and her wealthy father, who lived so lonely and secluded at the Abbey, and whose ways were altogether so different from those of his father before him.

The Major listened to every syllable, and only edged-in a word or two now and then, when the conversation flagged, or when there was a chance of the subject being changed.

By this means he contrived to keep the Lisfordians constant to one topic all the evening, and that topic was the manners and customs of Henry Dunbar.

Very early on the morning of the wedding the

Major made his appearance in the churchyard. As for the incessant rain, that was nothing to *him;* he was used to it; and, moreover, the wet weather gave him a good excuse for buttoning his coat to the chin, and turning the poodle collar over his big red ears.

He found the door of the church ajar, early though it was, and going in softly, he came upon the Tory beadle and some damp charity-children.

The Major contrived to engage the Tory beadle in conversation, which was not very difficult, seeing that the aforesaid beadle was always ready to avail himself of any opportunity of hearing his own voice. Of course the loquacious beadle talked chiefly of Sir Philip Jocelyn and the banker's daughter; and again the sporting gentleman from London heard of Henry Dunbar's riches.

"I *have* heerd as Mr. Dunbar is the richest man in Europe, exceptin' the Hemperore of Roosia and Baron Rothschild," the beadle said; "but I don't know any think more than that he's got a deal more money than he knows what to do with, seein' that he passes the best part of his days sittin' over the fire in his own room, or ridin' out after dark on horseback, if report speaks correct."

"I tell you what I'll do," said the Major, "as I am in Lisford,—and, to be candid with you, Lisford's about the dullest place it was ever my bad luck to visit,—why, I'll stay and have a look at this wedding. I suppose you can put me into a quiet pew, back yonder in the shadow, where I can see all that's going on, without any of your fine folks seeing me, eh?"

As the Major emphasised this question by dropping half-a-crown into the beadle's hand, that official answered it very promptly—

"I'll put you into the comfortablest pew you ever sat in," answered the official.

"You might do that easily," muttered the sporting gentleman, below his breath; "for there's not many pews, or churches either, that *I've* ever sat in."

The Major took his place in a corner of the church whence there was a very good view of the altar, where the feeble flames of the wax-candles made little splashes of yellow light in the fog.

The fog got thicker and thicker in the church as the hour for the marriage ceremony drew nearer and nearer, and the light of the wax-candles grew brighter as the atmosphere became more murky.

The Major sat patiently in his pew, with his arms folded upon the ledge, where the prayer-books in the corner of the seats were wont to rest during divine service. He planted his bristly chin upon his folded arms, and closed his eyes in a kind of dog sleep.

But in this sleep he could hear every thing going on. He heard the hobnailed soles of the charity-children pattering upon the floor of the church; he heard the sharp rustling of the evergreens and wet flowers under the children's figures; and he could hear the deep voice of Philip Jocelyn, talking to the clergyman in the porch, as he waited the arrival of the carriages from Maudesley Abbey.

The carriages arrived at last; and presently the wedding train came up the narrow aisle, and took their places about the altar-rails. Henry Dunbar stood behind his daughter, with his face in shadow.

The marriage service was commenced. The Major's eyes were wide open now. Those sharp eager black eyes took notice of every thing. They rested now upon the bride, now upon the bridegroom, now upon the faces of the rector and his curate.

Sometimes those glittering eyes strove to pierce the gloom and to see the other faces, the faces that were further away from the flickering yellow light of the wax-candles; but the gloom was not to be pierced even by the sharpest eyes.

The Major could only see four faces;—the faces of the bride and bridegroom, the rector, and his curate. But by and by, when one of the clergymen asked the familiar question—"*Who giveth this woman to be married to this man?*" Henry Dunbar came forward into the light of the wax-candles, and gave the appointed answer.

The Major's folded arms dropped off the ledge, as if they had been suddenly paralysed. He sat, breathing hard and quick, and staring at Mr. Dunbar.

"Henry Dunbar?" he muttered to himself, presently—"Henry Dunbar!"

Mr. Dunbar did not again retire into the shadow. He remained during the rest of the ceremony standing where the light shone full upon his handsome face.

When all was over, and the bride and bridegroom had signed their names in the vestry, before admiring witnesses, the sporting gentleman rose and walked softly out of the pew, and along one of the obscure side aisles.

The wedding party passed out of the church porch. The Major followed slowly.

Philip Jocelyn and his bride went straight to the carriage that was to convey them back to the Abbey.

Dora Macmahon and the two pale bridesmaids, with areophane bonnets that had become hopelessly limp from exposure to that cruel rain, took their places in the second carriage. They were accompanied by Arthur Lovell, whom they looked upon with no very great favour; for he had been silent and melancholy throughout the drive from Maudesley Abbey to Lisford Church, and had stared at them with vacant indifference, while handing them out of the carriage with a mechanical kind of politeness that was almost insulting.

The two first carriages drove away from the churchyard gate, and the mud upon the high road splashed the closed windows of the vehicles as the wheels went round.

The third carriage waited for Henry Dunbar, and the crowd in the churchyard waited to see him get into it.

He had his foot upon the lowest step, and his hand upon the door, when the Major went up to him, and tapped him lightly upon the shoulder.

The spectators recoiled, aghast with indignant astonishment.

How dared this shabby-looking man, with clumsy boots that were queer about the heels, and a mangy fur collar, like the skin of an invalid French poodle, to his threadbare coat—how, in the name of all that is audacious, dared such a low person as this lay his dirty fingers upon the sacred shoulder of Henry Dunbar, of Dunbar,

Dunbar, and Balderby's banking-house, St. Gundolph Lane, City?

The millionaire turned, and grew as ashy pale at sight of the shabby stranger as he could have done if the sheeted dead had risen from one of the graves near at hand. But he uttered no exclamation of horror or surprise. He only shrank haughtily away from the Major's touch, as if there had been some infection to be dreaded from those dirty finger-tips.

"May I be permitted to know your motive for this intrusion, sir?" the banker asked, in a cold, repellent voice, looking the shabby intruder full in the eyes as he spoke.

There was something so resolute, so defiant, in the rich man's gaze, that it is a wonder the poor man did not shrink from encountering it.

But he did not: he gave back look for look.

"Don't say you've forgotten me, Mr. Dunbar," he said; "don't say you've forgotten a very old acquaintance."

This was spoken after a pause, in which the two men had looked at each other as earnestly as if each had been trying to read the inmost secrets of the other's soul.

"Don't say you've forgotten me, Mr. Dunbar," repeated the Major.

Henry Dunbar smiled. It was a forced smile, perhaps; but at any rate, it was a smile.

"I have a great many acquaintances," he said; "and I fancy you must have gone down in the world since I knew you, if I may judge from appearances."

The bystanders, who had listened to every word, began to murmur among themselves. "Yes, indeed, they should rather think so:—if ever this shabby stranger had known Mr. Dunbar, and if he was not altogether an impostor, he must have been a very different sort of person at the time of his acquaintance with the millionaire."

"When and where did I know you?" asked Henry Dunbar, with his eyes still looking straight into the eyes of the other man.

"Oh, a long time ago—a very long way off!"

"Perhaps it was—somewhere in India—up the country?" said the banker, very slowly.

"Yes, it was in India—up the country," answered the other.

"Then you won't find me slow to befriend you," said Mr. Dunbar. "I am always glad to be of service to any of my Indian acquaintances—even when the world has treated them badly. Get into my carriage, and I'll drive you home. I shall be able to talk to you by and by, when all this wedding business is over."

The two men seated themselves side by side upon the spring cushions of the banker's luxurious carriage; and the vehicle drove rapidly away, leaving the spectators in a rapture of admiration at Henry Dunbar's condescension to his shabby Indian acquaintance.

CHAPTER VIII.

AFTER THE WEDDING.

THE banker and the man who was called the Major talked to each other earnestly enough throughout the short drive between Lisford churchyard and Maudesley Abbey; but they spoke in low, confidential whispers, and their conversation was interlarded by all manner of strange phrases; the queer, outlandish words were Hindostanee, no doubt, and were by no means easy to comprehend.

As the carriage drove up to the grand entrance of the Abbey, the stranger looked out through the mud-spattered window.

"A fine place!" he exclaimed; "a splendid place!"

"What am I to call you here?" muttered Mr. Dunbar, as he got out of the carriage.

"You may call me any thing; so long as you do not call me when the soup is cold. I've a two-pair back in the neighbourhood of St. Martin's Lane, and I'm known *there* as Mr. Vavasor. But I'm not particular to a shade. Call me any thing that begins with a V. It's as well to stick to one initial, on account of one's linen."

From the very small amount of linen exhibited in the Major's toilet, a malicious person might have imagined that such a thing as a shirt was a luxury not included in that gentleman's wardrobe.

"Call me Vernon," he said: "Vernon is a good name. You may as well call me Major Vernon. My friends at the Corner—not the Piccadilly corner, but the corner of the waste ground at the back of Field Lane—have done me the honour to give me the rank of Major, and I don't see why I shouldn't retain the distinction. My proclivities are entirely aristocratic. I have no power of assimilation with the *canaille*. This is the sort of thing that suits me. Here I am in my element."

Mr. Dunbar had led his shabby acquaintance

into the low, tapestried room in which he usually sat. The Major rubbed his hands with a gesture of enjoyment as he looked at the evidences of wealth that were heedlessly scattered about the apartment. He gave a long sigh of satisfaction as he dropped with a sudden plump upon the spring cushion of an easy-chair on one side of the fireplace.

"Now, listen to me," said Mr. Dunbar. "I can't afford to talk to you this morning; I have other duties to perform. When they're over, I'll come and talk to you. In the mean time, you may sit here as long as you like, and have what you please to eat or drink."

"Well, I don't mind the wing of a fowl and a bottle of Burgundy. It's a long time since I've tasted Burgundy. Chambertin or Clos de Vougeot, at twelve bob a bottle—that's the sort of tipple, I rather flatter myself—eh?"

Henry Dunbar drew himself up with a slight shudder, as if repelled and disgusted by the man's vulgarity.

"What do you want of me?" he asked.

"Remember that I am waited for. I am quite ready to serve you—for the sake of—'auld lang syne.'"

"Yes," answered the Major, with a sneer; "it's so pleasant to remember 'auld lang syne!'"

"Well," asked Mr. Dunbar, impatiently, "what is it you want of me?"

"A bottle of Burgundy—the best you have in your cellar—something to eat, and—that which a poor man generally asks of his rich friends—his fortunate friends—MONEY!"

"You shall not find me illiberal towards you. I'll come back by and by, and write you a cheque."

"You'll make it a thumping one?"

"I'll make it as much as you want."

"That's the sort of thing. There always was something princely and magnificent about you, Mr. Dunbar."

"You shall not have any reason to complain," answered the banker, very coldly.

"You'll send me the lunch?"

"Yes. You can hold your tongue, I suppose? You won't talk to the servant who waits upon you?"

"Has your friend the manners of a gentleman, or has he not? Hasn't he had the eminent advantage of a collegiate education,—I may say, a prolonged course of collegiate study? But, look here, since you're so afraid of my putting my foot in it, suppose I go back to Lisford now, and I can return to you to-night after dark. Our business will keep. I want a long talk, and a quiet talk; but I must suit my convenience to yours. It's the dee-yuty of the poor-r-r dependent to wait upon the per-leasure of his patron," exclaimed Major Vernon, in the studied tones of the villain in a melodrama.

Henry Dunbar gave a sigh of relief.

"Yes, that will be much better," he said. "I can talk to you comfortably after dinner."

"Ta-ta, then, old boy. 'Oh, reservoir!' as we say in the classics."

Major Vernon extended a brawny hand of rather doubtful purity. The millionaire touched the broad palm with the tips of his gloved fingers.

"Good-bye," he said; "I shall expect you at nine o'clock. You know your way out?"

He opened the door as he spoke, and pointed through a vista of two or three adjoining rooms to the hall. It was rather a broad hint. The Major pulled the poodle collar still higher above his ears, and went out with only his nose exposed to the influence of the atmosphere.

Henry Dunbar shut the door, and walked to one of the windows. He leaned his forehead against the glass, and looked out, watching the tall figure of the Major, as he walked rapidly along the broad carriage-drive that skirted the lawn.

The banker watched his shabby acquaintance until Major Vernon was quite out of sight. Then he went back to the fireplace, dropped heavily into his chair, and gave a long groan. It was not a sigh, it was a groan—a groan that seemed to come from a bosom that was rent by all the agony of despair.

"This decides it!" he muttered to himself. "Yes, this decides it! I've seen it for a long time coming to a crisis! But *this* settles every thing."

He got up, passed his hand across his forehead and over his eyelids, like a man who has just been awakened from a long sleep; and then went to play his part in the grand business of the day.

There is a very wide difference between the feelings of the poor adventurer—who, by some lucky accident, is enabled to pounce upon a rich friend—and the sentiments of the wealthy victim who is pounced upon. Nothing could present a stronger contrast than the manner of Henry Dunbar the banker, and the gentleman who had elected to be called Major Vernon. Whereas Mr. Dunbar seemed plunged into the uttermost depths of despair by the sudden appearance of his old acquaintance, the worthy Major exhibited a delight that was almost uproarious in its manifestation.

It was not until he found himself in a very lonely part of the park, where there were no other witnesses than the timid deer, lurking here and there under the poor shelter of a clump of leafless elms,—it was not till Major Vernon felt himself quite alone, that he gave way to the full exuberance of his spirits.

"It's a gold-mine!" he cried, rubbing his hands; "it's a regular California!"

He executed a grim caper in his delight, and the scared deer fled away from the neighbourhood of his path; perhaps they took him for some modern gnome, dancing wild dances in the wet woodland. He laughed aloud, with a hollow, fiendish-sounding laugh, and then clapped his hands together till the noise of his brawny palms echoed in the rustic silence.

"Henry Dunbar," he said to himself; "Henry Dunbar! He'll be a milch cow—nothing but a milch cow. If—" he stopped suddenly, and the triumphant grin upon his face changed to a thoughtful expression. "If he doesn't run away," he said, standing quite still, and rubbing his chin slowly with the palm of his hand. "What if he should give me the slip? He *might* do that!"

But, after a moment's pause, he laughed aloud again, and walked on briskly.

"No, he'll not do that," he said; "it won't serve his turn to run away."

While Major Vernon went back to Lisford, Henry Dunbar took his seat at the breakfast-table, with Laura Lady Jocelyn by his side.

There was very little more gaiety at the wedding-breakfast than there had been at the wedding. Every thing was very elegant, very subdued, and aristocratic. Silent footmen glided noiselessly backwards and forwards behind the chairs of the guests; champagne, Moselle, hock, and Burgundy sparkled in shallow glasses that were shaped like the broad leaf of a water-lily. Dresden-china shepherdesses in the centre of the oval table held up their chintz-patterned aprons filled with some forced strawberries that had cost about half-a-crown a piece. Smirking shepherds supported open-work baskets, laden with tiny Algerian apples, China oranges, and big purple hothouse grapes.

The bride and bridegroom were very happy;

but theirs was a subdued and quiet happiness that had little influence upon those around them. The wedding-breakfast was a very silent meal, for the face of the giver of the feast was as gloomy as the sky above Maudesley Abbey; and every now and then, in awkward pauses of the conversation, the pattering of the incessant raindrops sounded upon the windows.

At last the breakfast was finished. A knife had been cunningly inserted in the outer-wall of the splendid cake, and a few morsels of the rich interior, which looked like a kind of portable Day and Martin, had been eaten by one of the bridesmaids. Laura Jocelyn rose and left the table, attended by the three young ladies.

Elizabeth Madden was waiting in the bride's dressing-room with Lady Jocelyn's travelling-dress laid in state upon a big sofa. She kissed her young Miss, and cried over her a little, before she was equal to begin the business of the toilette; and then the voices of the bridesmaids broke loose, and there was a pleasant buzz of congratulation, which beguiled the time while Laura was exchanging her bridal costume for a long rustling dress of dove-coloured silk, a purple-velvet cloak trimmed and lined with sable, and a miraculous fabric of pale-pink areophane, and starry jasmine-blossoms, which the Parisian milliner facetiously entitled "a bonnet."

She went downstairs presently in this rich attire, looking like a Russian empress, in all the glory of her youth and beauty. The travelling-carriage was standing at the door; Arthur Lovell and Mr. Dunbar were in the hall with the two clergymen. Laura went up to her father to bid him good-bye.

"It will be a long time before we see each other again, papa dear," she said, in tones that were only loud enough for Mr. Dunbar to hear; "say 'God bless you!' once more before I go."

Her head was on his breast, and her face lifted up towards his own as she said this.

The banker looked straight before him with a forced smile upon his face, that was little more than a nervous contraction of the muscles about the lips.

"I will give you something better than my blessing, Laura," he said aloud; "I have given you no wedding-present yet, but I have not forgotten. The gift I mean to present to you will take some time to prepare. I shall give you the handsomest diamond-necklace that was ever made in England. I shall buy the diamonds myself, and have them set according to my own design."

The bridesmaids gave a little murmur of delight.

Laura pressed the speaker's cold hand.

"I don't want any diamonds, papa," she whispered; "I only want your love!"

Mr. Dunbar did not make any response to that entreating whisper. There was no time for any answer perhaps, for the bride and bridegroom had to catch an appointed train at Shorncliffe station, which was to take them on the first stage of their Continental journey; and in the bustle and confusion of their hurried departure, the banker had no opportunity of saying any thing more to his daughter. But he stood in the Gothic porch, watching the departing carriage with a kind of mournful tenderness in his face.

"I hope that she will be happy," he muttered to himself, as he went back to the house. "Heaven knows I hope she may be happy."

He did not stop to make any ceremonious adieu to his guests, but walked straight to his own apartments. People were accustomed to his strange manners, and were very indulgent towards his foibles.

Arthur Lovell and the three bridesmaids lingered a little in the blue drawing-room. The Melvilles were to drive home to their father's house in the afternoon, and Dora Macmahon was going with them. She was to stay at their father's house for a few weeks, and was then to go back to her aunt in Scotland.

"But I am to pay my darling Laura an early visit at Jocelyn's Rock," she said, when Arthur made some inquiry about her arrangements; "that has been all settled."

The ladies and the young lawyer took an afternoon tea together before they left Maudesley, and were altogether very sociable, not to say merry. It was upon this occasion that Arthur Lovell, for the first time in his life, observed that Dora Macmahon had very beautiful brown eyes, and rippling brown hair, and the sweetest smile he had ever seen—except in one lovely face, which was like the splendour of the noonday sun, and seemed to extinguish all lesser lights.

The carriage was announced at last; and Mr. Lovell had enough to do in attending to the three young ladies, and the stowing away of all those bonnet-boxes, and shawls, and travelling-bags, and desks, and dressing-cases, and odd volumes of books, and umbrellas, parasols, and sketching-portfolios, which are the peculiar attributes of all female travellers. And then, when all was finished, and he had bowed for the last time in acknowledgment of those friendly becks and wreathed smiles which greeted him from the carriage-window till it disappeared in the curve of the avenue, Arthur Lovell walked slowly home, thinking of the business of the day.

Laura was lost to him for ever. The dreadful

grief which had so long brooded darkly over his life had come down upon him at last, and the pang had not been so insupportable as he had expected it to be.

"I never had any hope," he thought to himself, as he walked along the soddened road between the gates of Maudesley and the old town that lay before him. "I never really hoped that Laura Dunbar would be my wife."

John Lovell's house was one of the best in the town of Shorncliffe. It was a queer old house, with a sloping roof, and gable-ends of solid oak, adorned here and there by grim devices, carved by a skilful hand. It was a large house; but low and straggling; and unpretending in its exterior. The red light of a fire was shining in a wainscoted chamber, half sitting-room, half library. The crimson curtains were not yet drawn across the diamond-paned window. Arthur Lovell looked into the room as he passed, and saw his father sitting by the fire, with a newspaper at his feet.

There was no need to bolt doors against thieves

and vagabonds in such a quiet town as Shorncliffe. Arthur Lovell turned the handle of the street-door and went in. The door of his father's sitting-room was ajar, and the lawyer heard his son's step in the hall.

"Is that you, Arthur?" he asked.

"Yes, father," the young man answered, going into the room.

"I want to speak to you very particularly. I suppose this wedding at Maudesley Abbey has put all serious business out of your head."

"What serious business, father?"

"Have you forgotten Lord Herriston's offer?"

"The offer of the appointment in India? Oh, no, father; I have not forgotten, only—"

"Only what?"

"I have not been able to decide."

As he spoke, Arthur Lovell thought of Laura Dunbar. No; she was Laura Jocelyn now. It was a hard thing for the young man to think of her by that new name. Would it not be better for him to go away—to put immeasurable distance between himself and the woman he had loved so dearly? Would it not be better and wiser to go away? And yet what if by so doing he turned his back upon another chance of happiness? What if a lesser star than that which had gone down in the darkness might be now rising dim and distant in the pale gray sky?

"There is no reason that I should decide in a hurry," the young man said, presently. "Lord Herriston told you that I might take twelve months to think about his offer."

"He did," answered John Lovell; "but half of the time is gone, and I've had a letter from Lord Herriston by this afternoon's post. He wants your decision immediately; for a connexion of his own has applied to him for the appointment. He still holds to his promise, and will give you the preference; but you must make up your mind at once."

"Do you wish me to go to India, father?"

"Do I wish you to go to India! Of course not, my dear boy, unless your own ambition takes you there. Remember, you are an only son. You have no occasion to leave this place. You will inherit a very good practice and a comfortable fortune. I thought you were ambitious, and that Shorncliffe was too narrow a sphere for your ambition, or else I should never have entertained any idea of this Indian appointment."

"And you will not be sorry if I remain in England?"

"Sorry! No, indeed; I shall be very glad. Do you suppose, when a man has only one son, a handsome, clever, high-minded young fellow, whose presence is like sunshine in his father's gloomy old house—do you think the father wants to get rid of the lad? If you do think so, you must have a very small idea of parental affection."

"Then I'll refuse the appointment, father."

"God bless you, my boy!" exclaimed the lawyer.

The letter to Lord Herriston was written that night; and Arthur Lovell resigned himself to a perpetual residence in that quiet town; within a mile of which the towers of Jocelyn's Rock crowned the tall cliff above the rushing waters of the Avon.

Mr. Dunbar had given all necessary directions for the reception of his shabby friend.

The Major was ushered at once to the tapestried room, where the banker was still sitting at the dinner-table. He had that meal laid upon a round table near the fire, and the room looked a very picture of comfort and luxury as Major Vernon went into it, fresh from the black, foggy night, and the leafless avenue, where the bare trunks of the elms looked like gigantic shadows looming through the obscurity.

The Major's eyes were almost dazzled by the brightness of that pleasant chamber. This man was a reprobate; but he had begun life as a gentleman. He remembered such a room as this long ago, across a dreary gulf of forty ill-spent years. The sight of this room brought back the memory of a pretty lamplit parlour, with an old man sitting in a high-backed easy-chair; a genial matron bending over her work; two fair-faced girls; a favourite mastiff stretched full length upon the hearth; and, last of all, a young man at home from college, yawning over a sporting newspaper, weary to death of all the simple innocent delights of home, sick of the companionship of gentle sisters, the love of a fond mother, and wishing to be back again at the old uproarious wine-parties, the drunken orgies, the card-playing and prize-fighting, the extravagance and debauchery of the bad set in which he was a chief.

The Major gave a profound sigh as he looked round the room. But the melancholy shadow on his face changed into a grim smile, as he glanced from the tapestried walls and curtained window, with a great Indian jar of hot-house flowers standing upon an inlaid table before it, and filling the room with a faint perfume of jasmine and almond, to the figure of Henry Dunbar.

"It's comfortable," said Major Vernon; "to say the least of it, it's very comfortable. And with a balance of half a million or so at one's banker's, or in one's own bank,—which is better still, perhaps,—one is not so badly off, eh, Mr. Dunbar?"

"Sit down and eat one of those birds," answered the banker. "I'll talk to you by and by."

The Major obeyed his friend; he unwound three or four yards of dingy woollen stuff from his scraggy throat, turned down the poodle collar, pulled his chair close to the table, squared his elbows, and began business. He made very light of a brace of partridges and a bottle of sparkling Moselle.

When the table had been cleared, and the two men left alone together, Major Vernon stretched his long legs upon the hearthrug, plunged his hands deep down in his trousers-pockets, and gave a sigh of satisfaction.

"And now," said Mr. Dunbar, filling his glass from the starry crystal claret-jug, "what is it that you want to say to me, Stephen Vallance, or Major Vernon, or whatever ridiculous name you may call yourself;—what is it you've got to say?"

"I'll tell you that in a very few words," answered the Major, quietly; "I want to talk to you about the man who was murdered at Winchester some months ago!"

The banker's hand lost its steadiness, the neck of the claret-jug knocked against the thin lip of the glass, and shivered it into half-a-dozen pieces.

"You'll spill your wine," said Major Vernon. "I'm very sorry for you if your nerves are no better than that."

When Major Vernon that night left his friend, he carried away with him half-a-dozen cheques for different amounts, making in all two thousand pounds, upon that private banking-account which Mr. Dunbar kept for himself in the house of Dunbar, Dunbar, and Balderby.

It was after midnight when the banker opened the hall-door, and passed out with the Major upon the broad stone flags, under the Gothic porch. There was no rain now; but it was very dark, and the north-easterly winds were blowing amongst the leafless branches of giant oaks and elms.

"Shall you present those cheques yourself?" Henry Dunbar asked, as the two men were about to part.

"Yes, I think so."

"Dress yourself decently, then, before you do so," said the banker; "they'd wonder what dealings you and I could have together, if you were to show yourself in St. Gundolph Lane in your present costume."

"My friend is proud," exclaimed the Major, with a mock tragic accent; "he is proud, and he despises his humble dependent."

"Good night," said Mr. Dunbar, rather abruptly; "it's past twelve o'clock, and I'm tired."

"To be sure. You're tired. Do you—do you—sleep well?" asked Major Vernon, in a whisper. There was no mock solemnity in his tone now.

The banker turned away from him with a muttered oath. The light of a lamp suspended from the groined roof of the porch shone upon the two men's faces. Henry Dunbar's countenance was overclouded by a black frown, and was by no means agreeable to look upon; but the grinning face of the Major, the thin lips wreathed into a malicious smile, the small black eyes glittering with a sinister light, looked like the face of a Mephistopheles.

"Good night," repeated the banker, turning his back upon his friend, and about to reënter the house.

Major Vernon laid his bony fingers upon Henry Dunbar's shoulder, and stopped him before he could cross the threshold.

"You've given me two thou'," he said; "that's liberal enough to start with; but I'm an old man; I'm tired of the life of a vagabond, and I want to live like a gentleman;—not as you do, of course; *that*'s out of the question; it isn't every body that has the good luck to be a millionaire, like Henry Dunbar; but I want a bottle of claret with my dinner, a good coat upon my back, and a five-pound note in my pocket constantly. You must do as much as that for me; eh, dear boy?"

"I don't refuse to do it, do I?" asked Henry Dunbar, impatiently; "I should think what you've got in your pocket already is a pretty good beginning."

"My dear fellow, it's a stupendous beginning!" exclaimed Major Vernon; "it's a princely beginning; it's a Napoleonic beginning. But that two thou' isn't meant for a blind, is it? It's not to be the beginning, middle, and the end? You're not going to do the gentle bolt —eh?"

"What do you mean?"

"You're not going to run away? You're not going to renounce the pomps and vanities of this wicked world, and make an early expedition across the herring-pond—eh, friend of my soul?"

"Why should I run away?" asked Henry Dunbar, sternly.

"That's the very thing I say myself, dear boy. Why should you? A wise man doesn't run away from landed estates, and fine houses, and half a million of money. But when you broke that claret-glass after dinner, it struck me somehow that you were — shall I venture the word?—*rather* nervous! Nervous people do all manner of things. Give me your word that you're not going to bolt, and I'm satisfied."

"I tell you, I have no such idea in my mind," Mr. Dunbar answered, with increasing impatience. "Will that do?"

"It will, dear boy. Your hand upon it! What a cold hand you've got! Take care of yourself; and once more—good night!"

"You're going to London?"

"Yes—to cash the cheques, and make a few business arrangements."

Mr. Dunbar bolted the great door as the footsteps of his friend the Major died away upon the gravelled walk, which had been quickly dried by the frosty wind. The banker had dismissed his servants at ten o'clock that night; so there was nobody to wait upon him, or to watch him, when he went back to the tapestried room.

He sat by the low fire for a little time, thinking, with a settled gloom upon his face, and drinking Burgundy out of a tumbler. Then he went to bed; and the light of the night-lamp shining upon his face as he slept, showed it distorted by strange shadows, that were not altogether the shadows of the draperies above his bed.

Major Vernon walked briskly down the long avenue leading to the lodge-gates.

"Two thou' is comfortable," he muttered to himself; "very satisfactory for a first go-in at the gold-diggin's! but I shall expect my California to produce a little more than that before we close the shaft, and retire upon the profits of the speculation. I *think* my friend is safe—I don't think he'll run away. But I shall keep my eye upon him, nevertheless. The human eye is a great institution; and I shall watch my friend."

In spite of a natural eagerness to transform those oblong slips of paper—the cheques signed with the well-known name of Henry Dunbar—into the still more convenient and flimsy paper circulating medium dispensed by the Old Lady in Threadneedle Street, or the yellow coinage of the realm, Major Vernon did not seem in any very great hurry to leave Lisford.

A great many of the Lisfordians had seen the shabby stranger take his seat in Henry Dunbar's carriage, side by side with the great banker. This fact became universally known throughout the parish of Lisford and two neighbouring parishes, before the shadows of night came down upon the day of Laura Dunbar's wedding, and the Major was respected accordingly.

He was shabby, certainly; queer about the heels of his boots; and very mangy with regard to the poodle collar. His hat was more shiny than was consistent with the hat-manufacturing interest. His bony hands were red and bare, and only one miserable mockery of a glove dangled between his thumb and finger as he swaggered along the village street.

But he had been seen riding in Henry Dunbar's carriage, and from that moment he had become invested with a romantic interest. He was a reduced gentleman, who had seen better days; or he was a miser, perhaps—an eccentric individual, who wore shabby boots and shiny hats for his own love and pleasure.

People paid respect, therefore, to the stranger at the Rose and Crown, and touched their hats to him as he went in and out, and were glad to answer any questions he chose to put to them as he loitered about the village.

He contrived to find out a good deal in this way about things in general and the habits of Henry Dunbar in particular. The banker had given his shabby acquaintance a handful of sovereigns for present use, as well as the cheques; and the Major was able to live upon the best the Rose and Crown could afford, and pay liberally for all he consumed.

"I find the Warwickshire air agree with me remarkably well," he said to the landlord, as he sat at breakfast in the bar-parlour, upon the second day after his interview with Henry Dunbar; "and if you know of any snug little box in the neighbourhood that would suit a lonely old bachelor with a comfortable income, and nobody to help him spend it, why, I really should have a very great inclination to take it, and furnish it."

The landlord scratched his head, and reflected for a few minutes. Then he slapped his leg with a sounding and triumphant slap.

"I know the very thing as would suit you, Major Vernon," he said—the Major had assumed the name of Vernon, as agreed upon between himself and Henry Dunbar—"the very thing," repeated the landlord; "you might say it had been made to order like. There's a sale comes off next Thursday. Mr. Grogson, the Shorncliffe auctioneer, will sell, at eleven o'clock precisely, the furniture and lease of the snuggest little box in these parts—Woodbine Cottage it's called—a sweet pretty little place, as was the property of old Admiral Manders. The admiral died in the house, and having been a bachelor, and his money having gone to distant relatives, the lease and furniture of the cottage will be sold. But I should think," added the landlord, gravely, looking rather doubtfully at his guest as he spoke, "I should think the lease and furniture, pictures and plate, will fetch a matter of eight hundred to a thousand pound; and perhaps you mightn't care to go to that?"

The landlord could not refrain from glancing furtively at the white and shining aspect of the cloth that covered the sharp knees of his customer, which were exactly under his eyes as the two men sat opposite to each other beside the snug little round table.

"You mightn't care to go to that price," he repeated, as he helped himself to about three-quarters of a pound of cold ham.

The Major lifted his bristly eyebrows with a contemptuous twitch.

"If the cottage suits me," he said, "I don't mind a thousand for it. To-day's Saturday;—I shall run up to town to-morrow, or Monday morning, to settle a bit of business I've got on hand, and come back here in time to attend the sale."

"My wife and me was thinkin' of goin', sir," the landlord answered, with unwonted reverence in his voice; "and, if it was agreeable, we could drive you over in our four-wheel shay. Woodbine Cottage is about a mile and a half from here, and little better than a mile from Maudesley Abbey. There's a copper coal-scuttle of the old admiral's as my wife has got rather a fancy for. But p'raps if you was to make a hoffer previous to the sale, the property might be disposed of as it stands by private contrack."

"I'll see about that," answered Major Vernon. "I'll stroll over to Shorncliffe this morning, and look in upon Mr. Grogson—Grogson, I think you said was the auctioneer's name?"

"Yes, sir; Peter Grogson, and very much looked up to he is, and a warm man, folks do say. His offices is in Shorncliffe High Street, sir; next door but two from Mr. Lovell's the solicitor's, and not more than half-a-dozen yards from St. Gwendoline's Church."

Major Vernon, as he now chose to call himself, walked from Lisford to Shorncliffe. He was a very good walker, and, indeed, had become pretty well used to pedestrian exercise in the course of long weary trampings from one race-course to another, when he was so far down on his luck as to be unable to pay his railway fare. The frost had set in for the first time this year; so the roads were dry and hard once more, and the sound of horses' hoofs and rolling wheels, the jingling of bells, the occasional barking of a noisy sheep-dog, and sturdy labourers' voices calling to each other on the high road, travelled far in the thin frosty air.

The town of Shorncliffe was very quiet to-day, for it was only on market-days that there was much life or bustle in the queer old streets, and Major Vernon found no hindrance to the business that had brought him from Lisford.

He went straight to Mr. Grogson the auctioneer, and from that gentleman heard all particulars respecting the pending sale at Woodbine Cottage. The Major offered to take the lease at a fair price, and the furniture, as it stood, by valuation.

"All I want is a comfortable little place that I can jump into without any trouble to myself," Major Vernon said, with the air of a man of the world. "I like to take life easily. If you can honestly recommend the place as worth seven or eight hundred pounds, I'm willing to pay that money for it down on the nail. I'll take it at your valuation, if the present owners are agreeable to sell it on those terms; and I'll pay a deposit of a couple of hundred or so on Tuesday afternoon, to show that my proposition is a *bona-fide* one."

A little more was said, and then Mr. Grogson pledged himself to act for the best in the interests of Major Vernon, consistently with his allegiance to the present owners of the property.

The auctioneer had been at first a little doubtful of this tall, shabby stranger in the napless dirty-white beaver and the mangy poodle collar; but the offer of a deposit of two hundred pounds or so gave a different aspect to the case. There are always eccentric people in the world, and appearances are very apt to be deceptive. There was a confident air about the Major which seemed like that of a man with a balance at his banker's.

The Major went back to the Rose and Crown, ate a comfortable little dinner, which he had ordered before setting out for Shorncliffe, paid his bill, and made all arrangements for starting by the first train for London on the following morning. It was nearly ten o'clock by the time he had done this; but late as it was, Major Vernon put on his hat, turned his poodle collar up about his ears, and went out into Lisford High Street.

There was scarcely one glimmer of light in the street as the Major walked along it. He took the road leading to Maudesley Abbey, and walked at a brisk pace, heedless of the snow, which was still falling thick and fast.

He was covered from head to foot with snow when he stopped before the stone porch, and rang a bell, that made a clanging noise in the stillness of the night. He looked like some grim white statue that had descended from its pedestal to stalk hither and thither in the darkness.

The servant who opened the door yawned undisguisedly in the face of his master's friend.

"Tell Mr. Dunbar that I shall be glad to speak to him for a few minutes," the Major said, making as if he would have passed into the hall.

"Mr. Dunbar left the habbey uppards of a *h*our ago," the footman answered, with supreme hauteur; "but he left a message for you, in case you was to come. The period of his habsence is huncertain, and if you wants to kermoonicate with him, you was to please to wait till he come back."

Major Vernon pushed aside the servant, and strode into the hall. The doors were open, and through two or three intermediate rooms the Major saw the tapestried chamber, dark and empty.

There was no doubt that Henry Dunbar had given him the slip—for the time, at least; but did the banker mean mischief? was there any deep design in this sudden departure?—that was the question.

"I'll write to your master," the Major said, after a pause; "what's his London address?"

"Mr. Dunbar left no address."

"Humph! That's no matter. I can write to him at the bank. Good night."

Major Vernon stalked away through the snow. The footman made no response to his parting civility, but stood watching him for a few moments, and then closed the door with a bang.

"Hif that's a spessermin of your Hinjun acquaintances, I don't think much of Hinjur or

Hinjun serciety; but what can you expect of a nation as insults the gentleman who waits behind his employer's chair at table by callin' him a kittenmüncher?"

CHAPTER IX.

WHAT HAPPENED IN THE BACK PARLOUR OF THE BANKING-HOUSE.

HENRY DUNBAR arrived in London a couple of hours after Mr. Vernon left the Abbey. He went straight to the Clarendon Hotel. He had no servant with him, and his luggage consisted only of a portmanteau, a dressing-case, and a despatch-box; the same despatch-box whose contents he had so carefully studied at the Winchester hotel, upon the night of the murder in the grove.

The day after his arrival was Sunday, and all that day the banker occupied himself in reading a morocco-bound manuscript volume, which he took from the despatch-box.

There was a black fog upon this November day, and the atmosphere out of doors was cold and bleak. But the room in which Henry Dunbar sat looked the very picture of comfort and elegance.

He had drawn his chair close to the fire, and on a table near his elbow were arranged the open despatch-box, a tall crystal jug of Burgundy, with a goblet-shaped glass, on a salver, and a case of cigars.

Until long after dark that evening, Henry Dunbar sat by the fire, smoking and drinking, and reading the manuscript volume. He only paused now and then to take pencil-notes of its contents in a little memorandum-book, which he carried in the breast-pocket of his coat.

It was not till seven o'clock, when the liveried servant who waited upon him came to inform him that his dinner was served in an adjoining chamber, that Mr. Dunbar rose from his seat and put away the book in the despatch-box. He laid down the volume on the table while he replaced other papers in the box, and it fell open at the first page. On that first page was written, in Henry Dunbar's bold, legible hand—

"*Journal of my life in India, from my arrival in* 1815, *until my departure in* 1850."

This was the book the banker had been studying all that winter's day.

At twelve o'clock the next day he ordered a brougham, and was driven to the banking-house in St. Gundolph Lane. This was the first time that Henry Dunbar had visited the house in St. Gundolph Lane since his return from India.

Those who knew the history of the present chief partner of the house of Dunbar, Dunbar, and Balderby, were in nowise astonished by this fact. They knew that, as a young man, Henry Dunbar had contracted the tastes and habits of an aristocrat, and that, if he had afterwards developed into a clever and successful man of business, it was only by reason of the force of circumstances, which had thrust him into a position that he hated.

It was by no means wonderful, then, that, after becoming possessor of the united fortunes of his father and his uncle, Henry Dunbar should keep aloof from a place that had always been obnoxious to him. The business had gone on without him very well during his absence, and it went on without him now, for his place in India had been assumed by a very clever man, who for twenty years had acted as cashier in the Calcutta house.

It may be that the banker had an unpleasant recollection of his last visit to St. Gundolph Lane, upon the day when the existence of the forged bills was discovered by Percival and Hugh Dunbar. All the width of thirty-five years between the present hour and that day might not be wide enough to separate the memory of the past from the thoughts which were busy this morning in the mind of Henry Dunbar.

Be it as it might, Mr. Dunbar's reflections this day were evidently not of a pleasant nature. He was very pale as he rode citywards, in the comfortable brougham, from the Clarendon; and his face had a stern, fixed look, like a man who has nerved himself to meet some crisis, which he knows is near at hand.

There was a stoppage upon Ludgate Hill. Great wooden barricades and mountains of uprooted paving-stones, amidst which sturdy navigators disported themselves with spades and pickaxes, and wheelbarrows full of rubbish blocked the way; so the brougham turned into Farringdon Street, and went up Snow Hill, and under the grim black walls of dreadful Newgate.

The vehicle travelled very slowly, for the traffic was concentrated in this quarter, by reason of the stoppage on Ludgate Hill; and Mr. Dunbar was able to contemplate at his leisure the black prison-walls, and the men and women selling dogs'-collars under their dismal shadows.

It may be that the banker's face grew a shade paler after that contemplation. The corners of his mouth twitched nervously as he got out of the carriage before the mahogany doors of the banking-house in St. Gundolph Lane. But he drew a long breath, and held his head proudly erect, as he pushed open the doors and went in.

Never since the day of the discovery of the forged bills had that man entered the banking-house. Dark thoughts came back upon his mind, and the shadows deepened on his face, as he gave one rapid glance round the familiar office.

He walked straight towards the private parlour in which that well-remembered scene had occurred five-and-thirty years ago. But before he arrived at the door leading from the public offices to the back of the house, he was stopped by a gentlemanly-looking man, who came forward from a desk in some shadowy region, and intercepted the stranger.

This man was Clement Austin the cashier.

"Do you wish to see Mr. Balderby, sir?" he asked.

"Yes. I have an appointment with him at one o'clock. My name is Dunbar."

The cashier bowed and opened the door. The banker passed across the threshold, which he had not crossed for five-and-thirty years until to-day.

But as Mr. Dunbar went towards the familiar parlour at the back of the banking-house, he stopped for a minute, and looked at the cashier.

Clement Austin was scarcely less pale than Henry Dunbar himself. He had heard of the banker's intended visit to St. Gundolph Lane, and had looked forward with strange anxiety to a meeting with the man whom Margaret Wilmot declared to be the murderer of her father. Now that the meeting had come to pass, he looked at Henry Dunbar with an earnest, scrutinising gaze: as if he would fain have discovered the secret of the man's guilt or innocence in his countenance.

The banker's face was pale, and grave, and stern: but Clement Austin knew that for Henry Dunbar there were very humiliating and unpleasant circumstances connected with the offices in St. Gundolph Lane: and it was scarcely to be expected that a man would come smiling into a place out of which he had gone five-and-thirty years before a disgraced and degraded creature.

For a few moments the two men paused in the passage between the public offices and the private parlour, looking at each other.

The banker's gaze never flinched during that encounter. It is taken as a strong proof of a man's innocence that he should look you full in the face with a steadfast gaze, when you look at him with suspicion plainly visible in your eyes: but would he not be the poorest villain if he shirked that encounter of glances, when he knows full surely that he is in that moment put to the test? It is rather innocence whose eyelids drop when you peer too closely into its eyes: for innocence is appalled by the stern, accusing glances which it is unprepared to meet. Guilt stares you boldly in the face: for guilt is hardened and defiant, and has this one grand superiority over innocence—that it is *prepared for the worst.*

Clement Austin opened the door of Mr. Balderby's parlour; Mr. Dunbar went in unannounced. The cashier closed the parlour-door, and returned to his desk in the public office.

The junior partner was sitting at an office-table near the fire, writing; but he rose as the banker entered the room, and went forward to meet him.

"You are very punctual, Mr. Dunbar," he said.

"Yes, I am generally punctual."

The two men shook hands, and Mr. Balderby wheeled forward a morocco-covered arm-chair for his senior partner, and then took his seat opposite to him, with only the small office-table between them.

"It may seem late in the day to bid you welcome to the Bank, Mr. Dunbar," said the junior partner; "but I do so, nevertheless—most heartily!"

There was a flatness in the accent in which these two last words were spoken, which was like the sound of a false coin when it falls dead upon a counter and proclaims itself spurious.

Henry Dunbar did not return his partner's greeting. He was looking round the room, and remembering the day upon which he had last seen it. There was very little alteration in the appearance of the dismal City chamber. There was the same wire-blind before the window, the same solitary tree, leafless, in the narrow courtyard without. The morocco-covered arm-chairs had been re-covered, perhaps, during that five-and-thirty years; but if so, the covering had grown shabby again. Even the Turkey carpet was in the very stage of dusty dinginess that had distinguished the carpet on which Henry Dunbar had stood five-and-thirty years before.

"I received your letter announcing your journey to London, and your desire for a private interview, on Saturday afternoon," Mr. Balderby said, after a pause. "I have made arrangements to assure our being undisturbed so long as you may remain here. If you wish to make any investigation of the affairs of the house, I—"

Mr. Dunbar waved his hand with a deprecatory air.

"Nothing is further from my thoughts than any such design," he said. "No, Mr. Balderby, I have only been a man of business because all chance of another career, which I infinitely preferred, was closed upon me five-and-thirty years ago. I am quite content to be a sleeping-partner in the house of Dunbar, Dunbar, and Balderby. For ten years prior to my father's death, he took no active part in the business. The house got on very well without his aid; it will get on equally well without mine. The business that brings me to London is an entirely personal matter. I am a rich man, but I don't exactly know how rich I am, and I want to realise rather a large sum of money."

Mr. Balderby bowed, but his eyebrows went

up a little, as if he found it impossible to control some slight evidence of his surprise.

"Previous to my daughter's marriage, I settled upon her the house in Portland Place and the Yorkshire property. She will have all my money when I die; and, as Sir Philip Jocelyn is a rich man, she will perhaps be one of the wealthiest women in England. So far so good. Neither Laura nor her husband will have any reason for dissatisfaction. But this is not quite enough, Mr. Balderby. I am not a demonstrative man, and I have never made any great fuss about my love for my daughter: but I do love her, nevertheless."

Mr. Dunbar spoke very slowly here, and stopped once or twice to pass his handkerchief across his forehead, as he had done in the hotel at Winchester.

"We Anglo-Indians have rather a magnificent way of doing things, Mr. Balderby," he continued, "when we take it into our heads to do them at all. I want to give my daughter a diamond-necklace as a wedding present, and I want it to be such as an eastern prince or a Rothschild might offer to his only child. You understand?"

"Oh, perfectly," answered Mr. Balderby; "I shall be most happy to be of any use to you in the matter."

"All I want is a large sum of money at my command. I may go rather recklessly to work, and make a large investmént in this necklace; it will be something for Lady Jocelyn to bequeath to her children. You and John Lovell, of Shorncliffe, were the executors to my father's will. You signed an order for the transfer of my father's money to my account some time in last September."

"I did, in concurrence with Mr. Lovell."

"Precisely; Lovell wrote me a letter to that effect. My father kept two accounts here, I believe—a deposit and a drawing account?"

"He did."

"And those two accounts have gone on since my return in the same manner as during his lifetime?"

"Precisely. The income which Mr. Percival

Dunbar set aside for his own use was seven thousand a year. He rarely spent as much as that; sometimes he spent less than half. The balance of this income, and his double share in the profits of the business, went to the credit of his deposit account, and various sums have been withdrawn from time to time, and duly invested under his order."

"Perhaps you can let me see the ledgers containing those two accounts?"

"Most certainly."

Mr. Balderby touched the spring of a handbell upon his table.

"Ask Mr. Austin to bring the daily balance and deposit accounts ledgers," he said to the person who answered his summons.

Clement Austin appeared five minutes afterwards, carrying two ponderous morocco-bound volumes.

Mr. Balderby opened both ledgers, and placed them before his senior partner. Henry Dunbar looked at the deposit account. His eyes ran eagerly down the long row of figures before him until they came to the sum-total. Then his chest heaved, and he drew a long breath, like a man who feels almost stifled by some internal oppression.

The last figures in the page were these:

137,926*l.* 17*s.* 2*d.*

One hundred and thirty-seven thousand nine hundred and twenty-six pounds seventeen shillings and twopence. The twopence seemed a ridiculous anti-climax; but business-men are necessarily as exact in figures as calculating-machines.

"How is this money invested?" asked Henry Dunbar, pointing to the page. His fingers trembled a little as he did so, and he dropped his hand suddenly upon the ledger.

"There's fifty thousand in India stock," Mr. Balderby answered, as indifferently as if fifty thousand pounds more or less was scarcely worth speaking of; "and there's five-and-twenty in railway debentures, Great Western. Most of the remainder is floating in exchequer bills."

"Then you can realise the exchequer bills?"

Mr. Balderby winced as if some one had trodden upon one of his corns. He was a banker heart and soul, and he did not at all relish the idea of any withdrawal of the bank's resources, however firm that establishment might stand.

"It's rather a large amount of capital to withdraw from the business," he said, rubbing his chin, thoughtfully.

"I suppose the bank can afford it!" Mr. Dunbar exclaimed, with a tone of surprise.

"Oh, yes; the bank can afford it well enough. Our calls are sometimes heavy. Lord Yarsfield—a very old customer—talks of buying an estate in Wales; he may come down upon us at any moment for a very stiff sum of money. However, the capital is yours, Mr. Dunbar; and you've a right to dispose of it as you please. The exchequer bills shall be realised immediately."

"Good; and if you can dispose of the railway bonds to advantage, you may do so."

"You think of spending—"

"I think of reinvesting the money. I have an offer of an estate north of the metropolis, which I think will realise cent per cent a few years hence: but that is an after consideration. At present we have only to do with the diamond-necklace for my daughter. I shall buy the diamonds myself, direct from the merchant-importers. You will hold yourself ready after Wednesday, we'll say, to cash some very heavy cheques on my account?"

"Certainly, Mr. Dunbar."

"Then I think that is really all I have to say. I shall be happy to see you at the Clarendon, if you will dine with me any evening that you are disengaged."

There was very little heartiness in the tone of this invitation; and Mr. Balderby perfectly understood that it was only a formula which Mr. Dunbar felt himself called upon to go through. The junior partner murmured his acknowledgment of Henry Dunbar's politeness; and then the two men talked together for a few minutes on indifferent subjects.

Five minutes afterwards Mr. Dunbar rose to leave the room. He went into the passage between Mr. Balderby's parlour and the public offices of the bank. This passage was very dark; but the offices were well lighted by lofty plate-glass windows. Between the end of the passage and the outer doors of the bank, Henry Dunbar saw the figure of a woman sitting near one of the desks and talking to Clement Austin.

The banker stopped suddenly, and went back to the parlour.

He looked about him a little absently as he reëntered the room.

"I thought I brought a cane," he said.

"I think not," replied Mr. Balderby, rising from before his desk. "I don't remember seeing one in your hand."

"Ah, then, I suppose I was mistaken."

He still lingered in the parlour, putting on his gloves very slowly, and looking out of the window into the dismal back-yard, where there was a dingy little wooden door set deep in the stone wall.

While the banker loitered near the window, Clement Austin came into the room to show some document to the junior partner. Henry Dunbar turned round as the cashier was about to leave the parlour.

"I saw a woman just now talking to you in the office. That's not very business-like, is it, Mr. Austin? Who is the woman?"

"She is a young lady, sir."

"A young lady?"

"Yes, sir."

"What brings her here?"

The cashier hesitated for a moment before he replied. "She—she wishes to see you, Mr. Dunbar," he said, after that brief pause.

"What is her name?—who—who is she?"

"Her name is Wilmot—Margaret Wilmot."

"I know no such person!" answered the banker, haughtily, but looking nervously at the half-opened door as he spoke.

"Shut that door, sir!" he said, impatiently, to the cashier; "the draught from the passage is strong enough to cut a man in two. Who is this Margaret Wilmot?"

"The daughter of that unfortunate man, Joseph Wilmot, who was cruelly murdered at Winchester!" answered the cashier, very gravely.

He looked Henry Dunbar full in the face as he spoke.

The banker returned his look as unflinchingly as he had done before, and spoke in a hard, unfaltering voice as he answered him:

"Tell this person, Margaret Wilmot, that I refuse to see her to-day, as I refused to see her in Portland Place, and as I refused to see her at Winchester!" he said, deliberately. "Tell her that I shall always refuse to see her, whenever or wherever she makes an attack upon me. I have suffered enough already on account of that hideous business at Winchester, and I shall most resolutely defend myself from any further persecution. This young person can have no possible motive for wishing to see me. If she is poor and wants money of me, I am ready and willing to assist her. I have already offered to do so—I can do no more. But if she is in distress—"

"She is not in distress, Mr. Dunbar," interrupted Clement Austin. "She has friends who love her well enough to shield her from that."

"Indeed; and you are one of those friends, I suppose, Mr. Austin?"

"I am."

"Prove your friendship, then, by teaching Margaret Wilmot that she has a friend and not an enemy in me. If you are—as I suspect from your manner—something more than a friend: if you love her, and she returns your love, marry her, and she shall have a dowry that no gentleman's wife need be ashamed to bring to her husband."

There was no anger, no impatience in the banker's voice now, but a tone of deep feeling. Clement Austin looked at him, astonished by this change in his manner.

Henry Dunbar saw the look, and it seemed as if he endeavoured to answer it.

"You have no need to be surprised that I shrink from seeing Margaret Wilmot," he said. "Cannot you understand that my nerves may be none of the strongest, and that I cannot endure the idea of an interview with this girl, who, no doubt, by her persistent pursuit of me, suspects *me* of her father's murder? I am an old man, and I have been thirty-five years in India. My health is shattered, and I have a horror of all tragic scenes. I have not yet recovered from the shock of that horrible business at Winchester. Go and tell Margaret Wilmot this: tell her that I will be her true friend if she will accept that friendship, but that I will not see her until she has learned to think better of me."

There was something very straightforward, very simple, in all this. For a time, at least, Clement Austin's mind wavered. Margaret was, perhaps, wrong, after all, and Henry Dunbar might be an innocent man.

It was Clement who had informed Margaret of Mr. Dunbar's expected presence here upon this day; and it was on the strength of that information that the girl had come to St. Gundolph Lane, with the determination of seeing the man whom she believed to be the murderer of her father.

Clement returned to the office, where he had left Margaret, in order to repeat to her Mr. Dunbar's message.

No sooner had the door of the parlour closed upon the cashier than Henry Dunbar turned abruptly to his junior partner.

"There is a door leading from the yard into a court that connects St. Gundolph Lane with another lane at the back," he said; "is there not?"

He pointed to the dark little yard outside the window as he spoke.

"Yes, there is a door, I believe."

"Is it locked?"

"No; it is seldom locked till four o'clock; the clerks use it sometimes, when they go in and out."

"Then I shall go out that way," said Mr. Dunbar, who was almost breathless in his haste. "You can send the carriage back to the Clarendon by and by. I don't want to see that girl. Good morning."

He hurried out of the parlour, and into a passage leading to the yard, followed by Mr. Balderby, who wondered at his senior partner's excitement. The door in the yard was not locked.

Henry Dunbar opened it, went out into the court, and closed the door behind him.

So, for the third time, he escaped from an interview with Margaret Wilmot.

CHAPTER X.

CLEMENT AUSTIN'S WOOING.

FOR the third time Margaret Wilmot was disappointed in the hope of seeing Henry Dunbar. Clement Austin had on the previous evening told her of the banker's intended visit to the office in St. Gundolph Lane, and the young music-mistress had made hasty arrangements for the postponement of her usual duties, in order that she might go to the City to see Henry Dunbar.

"He will not dare to refuse to see you," Clement Austin said; "for he must know that such a refusal would excite suspicion in the minds of the people about him."

"He must have known that at Winchester, and yet he avoided me there," answered Margaret Wilmot; "he must have known it when he refused to see me in Portland Place. He will refuse to see me to-day, if I ask for an interview with him. My only chance will be the chance of an accidental meeting with him. Do you think that you can arrange this for me, Mr. Austin?"

Clement Austin readily promised to bring about an apparently accidental meeting between Margaret and Mr. Dunbar, and this is how it was that Joseph Wilmot's daughter had waited in the office in St. Gundolph Lane. She had arrived only five minutes after Mr. Dunbar entered the banking-house, and she had waited very patiently, very resolutely, in the hope that when Henry Dunbar returned to his carriage she might snatch the opportunity of speaking to him, of seeing his face, and discovering whether he was guilty or not.

She clung to the idea that some indefinable expression of his countenance would reveal the fact of his guilt or innocence. But she could not dispossess herself of the belief that he was guilty. What other reason could there be for his persistant avoidance of her?

But, for the third time, she was baffled; and

she went home very despondently, haunted by the image of her dead father; while Henry Dunbar went back to the Clarendon in a common hack cab, which he picked up in Cornhill.

Margaret Wilmot found one of her pupils waiting in the pretty little parlour in the cottage at Clapham, and she was obliged to sit down to the piano and listen to a fantasia very badly played, keeping sharp watch upon the pupil's fingers, for an hour or so, before she was free to think her own thoughts.

Margaret was very glad when the lesson was over. The pupil was a vivacious young lady, who called her music-mistress "dear," and would have been glad to waste half an hour or so in an animated conversation about the last new style in bonnets, or the shape of the fashionable winter mantle, or the popular novel of the month. But Margaret's pale face seemed a mute appeal for compassion; so Miss Lamberton drew on her gloves, settled her bonnet before the glass over the mantel-piece, and tripped away.

Margaret sat by the little round table, with

an open book before her. But she could not read, though the volume was one that had been lent her by Clement, and though she took a peculiar pleasure in reading any book that was a favourite of his. She did not read; she only sat with her eyes fixed, and her face very pale, in the dim light of two candles that flickered in the draught from the window.

She was aroused from her despondent reverie by a double knock at the door below, and presently the neat little maid-servant ushered Mr. Austin into the room.

Margaret started up, a little confused at the advent of this unexpected visitor. It was the first time that Clement had ever called upon her alone. He had often been her guest; but, until to-night, he had always come under his mother's wing to see the pretty music-mistress.

"I am afraid I startled you, Miss Wilmot," he said.

"Oh, no; not at all," answered Margaret; "I was sitting here, quite idle, thinking—"

"Thinking of your failure of to-day, I suppose?"

"Yes."

There was a pause, during which Margaret seated herself once more by the little table, while Clement Austin walked up and down the room, thinking.

Presently he stopped suddenly, with his elbow leaning upon the corner of the mantel-piece, opposite Margaret, and looked down at the girl's thoughtful face. She had blushed when the cashier first entered the room; but she was very pale now.

"Margaret," said Clement Austin,—it was the first time he had called his mother's protégée by her Christian name, and the girl looked up at him with a surprised expression,—"Margaret, that which happened to-day makes me think that your conviction is only the horrible truth, and that Henry Dunbar, the sole surviving kinsman of those two men whom I learnt to honour and revere long ago, when I was a mere boy, is indeed guilty of your father's death. If so, the cause of justice demands that this man's crime should be brought to light. I am something of Shakespeare's opinion; I cannot but believe that 'murder will out,' somehow or other, sooner or later. But I think that, in this business, the police have been culpably supine. It seems as if they feared to handle the case too closely, lest the clue they followed should lead them to Henry Dunbar."

"You think they have been bribed?"

"No; I don't think that. There seems to be a popular belief, all over the world, that a man with a million of money can do no wrong. I don't believe the police have been culpable; they have only been faint-hearted. They have suffered themselves to be discouraged by the difficulties of the case. Other crimes have been committed, other work has arisen for them to do, and they have been obliged to abandon an investigation which seemed hopeless. This is how criminals escape—this is how murderers are suffered to be at large; not because discovery is impossible, but because it can only be effected by a slow and wearisome process in which so few men have courage to persevere. While the country is ringing with the record of a great crime—while the murderer is on his guard night and day, waking and sleeping—

the police watch and work: but by and by, when the crime is half forgotten—when security has made the criminal careless—when the chances of detection are tenfold—the police have grown tired, and there is no eye to watch the guilty man's movements. I know nothing of the science of detection, Margaret; but I believe that Henry Dunbar was the murderer of your father; and I will do my uttermost, with God's help, to bring his crime home to him."

The girl's eyes flashed with a proud light, as Clement Austin finished speaking.

"Will you do this?" she said; "will you bring to light the mystery of my father's death? Will you bring punishment upon his murderer? It seems a horrible thing, perhaps, for a woman to wish detection to overtake any man, however base; but surely it would be more horrible if I were content to let my father's murder remain unavenged. My poor father! If he had been a good man, I do not think it would grieve me so much to remember his cruel death: but he was not a good man—he was not a good man."

"Let him have been what he may, Margaret, his murderer shall not go unpunished if I can aid the cause of justice," said Clement Austin. "But it was not to say this alone that I came here to-night, Margaret. I have something more to say to you."

There was a tenderness in the cashier's voice as he said these last words, that brought the blushes back to Margaret's pale cheeks.

"You *know* that I love you, Margaret," Clement said, in a low, earnest voice; "you must know that I love you: or if you do not, it is because there is no sympathy between us, and in that case my love is indeed hopeless. I have loved you from the first, dear—yes, from the very first summer twilight in which I saw your pale, pensive face in the dusky little garden at Wandsworth. The tender interest which I then felt in you was the first mysterious dawn of love, though I, in my infinite wisdom, put it down to an artistic admiration for your peculiar beauty. It was love, Margaret; and it has grown and strengthened in my heart ever since that summer evening, until it leads me here to-night to tell you all, and to ask you if there is any hope. Ah, Margaret, you must have known my love all along! You would have banished me had you felt that my love was hopeless: you could not have been so cruel as to deceive me."

Margaret looked up at her lover with a frightened face. Had she done wrong, then, to be happy in his society, if she did not love him—if she did not love him! But surely this sudden thrill of triumph and delight which filled her breast, as Clement spoke to her, must be in some degree akin to love.

Yes, she loved him; but the bright things of this world were not for her. Love and Duty fought for the mastery of her pure soul: and Duty was the conqueror.

"Oh, Clement!" she said, "do you forget who I am? Do you forget that letter which I showed you long ago, the letter addressed to my father when he was a transported felon, suffering the penalty of his crime? Do you forget who I am, and the taint that is in my blood; the disgrace that stains my name? I am proud to think that you have loved me, Clement Austin; but I am no fitting wife for you!"

"You are a noble, true-hearted woman, Margaret; and as such you are a fitting wife for a king. Besides, I am not such a grandee that I need look for high lineage in the wife of my choice. I am only a working man, content to accept a salary for my services; and looking forward by and by to a junior partnership in the house I serve. Margaret, my mother loves you; and she knows that you are the woman I seek to win as my wife. Forget the taint upon your dead father's name as freely as I forget it, dearest; and only answer me one question: Is my love hopeless?"

"I will never consent to be your wife, Mr. Austin!" Margaret answered in a low voice.

"Because you do not love me?"

"Because I will never cause you to blush for the history of your wife's girlhood."

"That is no answer to my question, Margaret," said Clement Austin, seating himself by her side, and taking both her hands in his. "I must ask you to look me full in the face, Miss Wilmot," he added, laughingly, drawing her towards him as he spoke; "for I begin to fancy you're addicted to prevarication. Look me in the face, Madge darling, and tell me that you love me."

But the blushing face would not be turned towards his own. Margaret's head was still averted.

"Don't ask me," she pleaded; "don't ask me. The day would come when you would regret your choice. I could not endure that. It would be too bitter. You have been very kind to me; and it would be a poor return for your kindness, if—"

"If you were to make me unutterably happy, eh, Margaret? I think it would be only a proper act of gratitude. Haven't I run all over Clapham, Brixton, and Wandsworth—to say nothing of an occasional incursion upon Putney—in order to procure you half-a-dozen pupils? And the very first favour I demand of you, which is only the gift of this clever little hand, you have the audacity to refuse me point-blank."

He waited for a few moments, in the hope that Margaret would say something; but her face was still averted, and the trembling hand which Mr. Austin was holding struggled to release itself from his grasp.

"Margaret," he said, very gravely, "perhaps I have been foolish and presumptuous in this business. In that case I fully deserve to be disappointed, however bitter the disappointment may be. If I have been wrong, Margaret; if I have been deceived by your sweet smiles, your gentle words; for pity's sake tell me that it is so, and I will forgive you for having involuntarily deceived me, and will try to cure myself of my folly. But I will not leave this room, I will not abandon the dear hope that has brought me here to-night, until you tell me plainly that you do not love me. Speak, Margaret, and speak fearlessly."

But Margaret was still silent, only in the silence Clement Austin heard a low sobbing sound.

"Margaret darling, you are crying. Ah! I

know now that you love me, and I will not leave this room except as your plighted husband."

"Heaven help me!" murmured Joséph Wilmot's daughter; "Heaven lead me right! for I do love you, Clement, with all my heart."

CHAPTER XI.

BUYING DIAMONDS.

Mr. Dunbar did not waste much time before he began the grand business which had brought him to London,—that is to say, the purchase of such a collection of diamonds as should compose a necklace second only to that which brought poor hoodwinked Cardinal de Rohan and the unlucky daughter of the Cæsars into such a morass of trouble and slander.

Early upon the morning after his visit to the bank, Mr. Dunbar went out very plainly dressed, and hailed the first empty cab that he saw in Piccadilly.

He ordered the cabman to drive straight to a street leading out of Holborn, a very quiet-looking street, where you could buy diamonds enough to set up all the jewellers in the Palais Royale and the Rue de la Paix, and where, if you were so whimsical as to wish to transform a service of plate into "white soup" at a moment's notice, you might indulge your fancy in establishments of unblemished respectability.

The gold and silver refiners, the diamond-merchants and wholesale jewellers, in this quiet street, were a very superior class of people, and you might dispose of a handful of gold chains and bangles without any fear that one or two of them would find their way into the operator's sleeve during the process of weighing. The great Mr. Krusible, who thrust the last inch of an eastern potentate's sceptre into the melting-pot with the sole of his foot, as the detectives entered his establishment in search of the missing bauble, and walked lame for six months afterwards, lived somewhere in the depths of the City, and far away from this dull-looking Holborn street; and would have despised the even tenor of life, and the moderate profits of a business in this neighbourhood.

Mr. Dunbar left his cab at the Holborn end of the street, and walked slowly along the pavement till he came to a very dingy-looking parlour-window, which might have belonged to a lawyer's office but for some gilded letters on the wire blind, which, in a very pale and faded inscription, gave notice that the parlour belonged to Mr. Isaac Hartgold, diamond-merchant. A grimy brass plate on the door of the house bore another inscription to the same effect; and it was at this door that Mr. Dunbar stopped.

He rang a bell, and was admitted immediately by a very sharp-looking boy, who ushered him into the parlour, where he saw a mahogany counter, a pair of small brass scales, a horsehair-cushioned office-stool considerably the worse for wear, and a couple of very formidable-looking iron safes deeply imbedded in the wall behind the counter. There was a desk near the window, at which a gentleman, with very black hair and whiskers, was seated, busily engaged in some abstruse calculations between a pair of open ledgers.

He got off his high seat as Mr. Dunbar entered, and looked rather suspiciously at the banker. I suppose the habit of selling diamonds had made him rather suspicious of every one. Henry Dunbar wore a fashionable greatcoat with loose open cuffs, and it was towards these loose cuffs that Mr. Hartgold's eyes wandered with rapid and rather uneasy glances. He was apt to look doubtfully at gentlemen with roomy coat-sleeves, or ladies with long-haired muffs or fringed parasols. Unset diamonds are an eminently portable species of property, and you might carry a tolerably valuable collection of them in the folds of the smallest parasol that ever faded under the summer sunshine in the ladies' mile.

"I want to buy a collection of diamonds for a necklace," Mr. Dunbar said, as coolly as if he had been talking of a set of silver spoons; "and I want the necklace to be something out of the common. I should order it of Garrard or Emanuel; but I have a fancy for buying the diamonds upon paper, and having them made up after a design of my own. Can you supply me with what I want?"

"How much do you want? You may have what some people would call a necklace for a thousand pounds, or you may have one that'll cost you twenty thousand. How far do you mean to go?"

"I am prepared to spend something between fifty and eighty thousand pounds."

The diamond-merchant pursed-up his lips reflectively. "You are aware that in these sort of transactions ready money is indispensable?" he said.

"Oh, yes, I am quite aware of that," Mr. Dunbar answered, coolly.

He took out his card-case as he spoke, and handed one of his cards to Mr. Isaac Hartgold. "Any cheques signed by that name," he said, "will be duly honoured in St. Gundolph Lane."

Mr. Hartgold bent his head reverentially to the representative of a million of money. He, in common with every business man in London, was thoroughly familiar with the names of Dunbar, Dunbar, and Balderby.

"I don't know that I can supply you with fifty thousand pounds' worth of such diamonds as you may require at a moment's notice," he said;

"but I can procure them for you in a day or two, if that will do?"

"That will do very well. This is Tuesday; suppose I give you till Thursday?"

"The stones shall be ready for you by Thursday, sir."

"Very good. I will call for them on Thursday morning. In the mean time, in order that you may understand that the transaction is a *bona-fide* one, I'll write a cheque for ten thousand, payable to your order, on account of diamonds to be purchased by me. I have my cheque-book in my pocket. Oblige me with pen and ink."

Mr. Hartgold murmured something to the effect that such a proceeding was altogether unnecessary; but he brought Mr. Dunbar his office inkstand, and looked on with an approving twinkle of his eyes while the banker wrote the cheque, in that slow, formal hand peculiar to him. It made things very smooth and comfortable, Mr. Hartgold thought, to say the least of it.

"And now, sir, with regard to the design of the necklace," said the merchant, when he had folded the cheque and put it into his waistcoat-pocket. "I suppose you've some idea that you'd like to carry out; and you'd wish, perhaps, to see a few specimens."

He unlocked one of the iron safes as he spoke, and brought out a lot of little paper packets, which were folded in a peculiar fashion, and which he opened with very gingerly fingers.

"I suppose you'd like some tallow-drops, sir?" he said. "Tallow-drops work-in better than any thing for a necklace."

"What, in heaven's name, are tallow-drops?"

Mr. Hartgold took up a diamond with a pair of pincers, and exhibited it to the banker.

"That's a tallow-drop, sir," he said. "It's something of a heart-shaped stone, you see; but we call it a tallow-drop, because it's very much the shape of a drop of tallow. You'd like large stones, of course, though they eat into a great deal of money? There are diamonds that are known all over Europe; diamonds that have been in the possession of royalty, and are as well known as the family they've belonged to. The Duke of Brunswick has pretty well cleared the market of that sort of stuff; but still they are to be had, if you've a fancy for any thing of that kind?"

Mr. Dunbar shook his head.

"I don't want any thing of that sort," he said; "the day may come when my daughter, or my daughter's descendants, may be obliged to realise the jewels. I'm a commercial man, and I want eighty thousand pounds' worth of diamonds that shall be worth the money I give for them to break up and sell again. I should wish you to choose diamonds of moderate size, but not small; worth, on an average, forty or fifty pounds a piece, we'll say."

"I shall have to be very particular about matching them in colour," said Mr. Hartgold, "as they're for a necklace."

The banker shrugged his shoulders.

"Don't trouble yourself about the necklace," he said, rather impatiently. "I tell you again I'm a commercial man, and what I want is good value for my money."

"And you shall have it, sir," answered the diamond-merchant, briskly.

"Very well, then; in that case I think we understand each other, and there's no occasion for me to stop here any longer. You'll have eighty thousand pounds' worth of diamonds, or thereabouts, ready for me when I call here on Thursday morning. You can cash that cheque in the mean time, and ascertain with whom you have to deal. Good morning."

He left the diamond-merchant wondering at his *sang froid*, and returned to the cab, which had been waiting for him all this time.

He was just going to step into it, when a hand touched him lightly on the shoulder, and turning sharply and angrily round, he recognised the gentleman who called himself Major Vernon.

But the Major was by no means the shabby stranger who had watched the marriage of Philip Jocelyn and Laura Dunbar in Lisford Church. Major Vernon had risen, resplendent as the phœnix, from the ashes of his old clothes.

The poodle collar was gone: the dilapidated

boots had been exchanged for stout water-tight Wellingtons: the napless dirty white hat had given place to a magnificent beaver, with a broad brim curled at the sides. Major Vernon was positively splendid. He was as much wrapped up as ever; but his wrappings now were of a gorgeous, not to say gaudy, description. His thick greatcoat was of a dark olive-green, and the collar turned up over his ears was of a shiny-looking brown fur, which, to the confiding mind of the populace, is known as imitation sable.

Inside this fur collar the Major wore a shawl-patterned scarf of all the colours in the prismatic scale, across which his nose lacked its usual brilliancy of hue by force of contrast. Major Vernon had a very big cigar in his mouth, and a very big cane in his hand, and the quiet City men turned to look at him as he stood upon the pavement talking to Henry Dunbar.

The banker writhed under the touch of his Indian acquaintance.

"What do you want with me?" he asked, in low angry tones; "why do you follow me about to play the spy upon me, and stop me in the public street? Haven't I done enough for you? Ain't you satisfied with what I have done?"

"Yes, dear boy," answered the Major, "perfectly satisfied, more than satisfied—for the present. But your future favours—as those low fellows, the butchers and bakers, have it—are respectfully requested for yours truly. Let me get into the cab with you, Mr. H. D., and take me back to the *casa*, and give me a comfortable little bit of per-rogg. I haven't lost my aristocratic taste for seven courses, and an elegant succession of still and sparkling wines, though during the last few years I've been rather frequently constrained to accept the shadowy hospitality of his grace of Humphrey. '*Nante dinari, nante manjare*,' as we say in the Classics, which I translate, 'No credit at the butcher's or the baker's.'"

"For Heaven's sake, stop that abominable slang," said Henry Dunbar, impatiently.

"It annoys you, dear friend, eh? Well, I've known the time when— But no matter, 'let what is broken, so remain,' as the poet observes;

which is only an elegant way of saying, Let bygones be bygones. And so you've been buying diamonds, dear boy?"

"Who told you so?"

"You did, when you came out of Mr. Isaac Hartgold's establishment. I happened to be passing the door as you went in, and I happened to be passing the door again as you came out."

"And playing the spy upon me."

"Not at all, dear boy. It was merely a coincidence, I assure you. I called at the bank yesterday, cashed my cheques, ascertained your address; called at the Clarendon this morning, was told you'd that minute gone out; looked down Albemarle Street; there you were, sure enough; saw you get into a cab; got into another—a Hansom, and faster than yours—came behind you to the corner of this street."

"You followed me," said Henry Dunbar, bitterly.

"Don't call it *following*, dear friend, because that's low. Accident brought me into this neighbourhood at the very hour you were coming into this neighbourhood. If you want to quarrel with any thing, quarrel with the doctrine of chances, not with me."

Henry Dunbar turned away with a sulky gesture. His friend watched him with very much the same malicious grin that had distorted his face under the lamp-lit porch at Maudesley. The Major looked like a vulgar-minded Mephistopheles: there was not even "the divinity of hell" about him.

"And so you've been buying diamonds?" he repeated presently, after a considerable pause.

"Yes, I have. I am buying them for a necklace for my daughter."

"You are so dotingly fond of your daughter!" said the Major, with a leer.

"It is necessary that I should give her a present."

"Precisely, and you won't even trust the business to a jeweller; you insist on doing it all yourself."

"I shall do it for less money than a jeweller."

"Oh, of course," answered Major Vernon; "the motive's as clear as daylight."

He was silent for a few minutes, then he laid his hand heavily upon his companion's shoulder, put his lips close to the banker's ear, and said, in a loud voice, for it was not easy for him to make himself heard above the jolting of the cab—

"Henry Dunbar, you're a very clever fellow, and, I daresay, you think yourself a great deal sharper than I am; but, by Heaven, if you try any tricks with me, you'll find yourself mistaken. You must buy me an annuity. Do you understand? Before you move right or left, or say your soul's your own, you must buy me an annuity!"

The banker shook off his companion's hand, and turned round upon him, pale, stern, and defiant.

"Take care, Stephen Vallance," he said; "take care how you threaten me. I should have thought you knew me of old, and would be wise enough to keep a civil tongue in your head, with *me.* As for what you ask, I shall do it, or I shall let it alone—as I think fit. If I do it, I shall take my own time about it, not yours."

"You're not afraid of me, then?" asked the other, recoiling a little, and much more subdued in his tone.

"No!"

"You are very bold."

"Perhaps I am. Do you remember the old story of some people who had a goose that laid golden eggs? They were greedy, and, in their besotted avarice, they killed the goose. But they have not gone down to posterity as examples of wisdom. No, Vallance, I'm not afraid of you."

Mr. Vallance leaned back in the cab, biting his nails savagely, and thinking. It seemed as if he was trying to find an answer for Mr. Dunbar's speech: but, if so, he must have failed, for he was silent for the rest of the drive: and when he got out of the vehicle, by and by, before the door of the Clarendon, his manner bore an undignified resemblance to that of a half-bred cur who carries his tail between his legs.

"Good afternoon, Major Vernon," the banker

said, carelessly, as a liveried servant opened the door of the hotel; "I shall be very much engaged during the few days I am likely to remain in town, and shall be unable to afford myself the pleasure of your society."

The Major stared aghast at this cool dismissal.

"Oh," he murmured vaguely, "that's it, is it? Well, of course, you know what's best for yourself—so, good afternoon!"

The door closed upon Major Vernon, alias Mr. Stephen Vallance, while he was still staring straight before him, in utter inability to realise his position. But he drew his cashmere shawl still higher up about his ears, took out a gaudy scarlet-morocco cigar-case, lighted another big cigar, and then strolled slowly down the quiet West-end street, with his bushy eyebrows contracted into a thoughtful frown.

"Cool!" he muttered between his closed lips; "very cool, to say the least of it. Some people would call it audacious. But the story of the goose with the golden eggs is one of childhood's simple lessons that we're obliged to remember in after life. And to think that the government of this country should have the audacity to offer a measly hundred pounds or so for the discovery of a great crime! The shabbiness of the legislature must answer for it, if criminals remain at large. My friend's a deep one, a cursedly deep one; but I shall keep my eye upon him. 'My faith is strong in time,' as the poet observes. My friend carries it with a high hand at present; but the day may come when he may want me; and if ever he does want me, egad, he shall pay me my own price, and it shall be rather a stiff one into the bargain."

CHAPTER XII.

GOING AWAY.

At one o'clock on the appointed Thursday morning, Mr. Dunbar presented himself in the diamond-merchant's office. Henry Dunbar was not alone. He had called in St. Gundolph Lane, and asked Mr. Balderby to go with him to inspect the diamonds he had bought for his daughter.

The junior partner opened his eyes to the widest extent as the brilliants were displayed before him, and declared that his senior's generosity was something more than princely.

But perhaps Mr. Balderby did not feel so entirely delighted two or three hours afterwards, when Mr. Isaac Hartgold presented himself before the counter in St. Gundolph Lane, whence he departed some time afterwards carrying away with him seventy-five thousand eight-hundred pounds in Bank-of-England notes.

Henry Dunbar walked away from the neighbourhood of Holborn with his coat buttoned tightly across his broad chest, and nearly eighty thousand pounds' worth of property hidden away in his breast-pockets. He did not go straight back to the Clarendon, but pierced his way across Smithfield, and into a busy smoky street, where he stopped by and by at a dingy-looking currier's shop.

He went in and selected a couple of chamois skins, very thick and strong. At another shop he bought some large needles, half-a-dozen skeins of stout waxed thread, a pair of large scissors, a couple of strong steel buckles, and a tailor's thimble. When he had made these purchases, he hailed the first empty cab that passed him, and went back to his hotel.

He dined, drank the best part of a bottle of Burgundy, and then ordered a cup of strong tea to be taken to his dressing-room. He had fires in his bed-room and dressing-room every night.

To-night he retired very early, dismissed the servant who attended upon him, and locked the door of the outer room, the only door communicating with the corridor of the hotel.

He drank a cup of tea, bathed his head with cold water, and then sat down at a writing-table near the fire.

But he was not going to write; he pushed aside the writing-materials, and took his purchases of the afternoon from his pocket. He spread the chamois leather out upon the table, and cut the skins into two long strips, about a foot broad. He measured these round his waist, and then began to stitch them together, slowly and laboriously.

The work was not easy, and it took the banker a very long time to complete it to his own satisfaction. It was past twelve o'clock when he had stitched both sides and one end of the double chamois-leather belt; the other end he left open.

When he had completed the two sides and the end that was closed, he took four or five little canvas-bags from his pocket. Every one of these canvas-bags was full of loose diamonds.

A thrill of rapture ran through the banker's veins as he plunged his fingers in amongst the glittering stones. He filled his hands with the bright gems, and let them run from one hand to the other, like streams of liquid light. Then, very slowly and carefully, he began to drop the diamonds into the open end of the chamois-leather belt.

When he had dropped a few into the belt, he stitched the leather across and across, quilting-in the stones. This work took him so long, that it was four o'clock in the morning when he had quilted the last diamond into the belt. He gave a long sigh of relief as he threw the waste scraps of leather upon the top of the low fire, and watched them slowly smoulder away into black ashes. Then he put the chamois-leather belt under his pillow, and went to bed.

Henry Dunbar went back to Maudesley Abbey by the express on the morning after the day on which he had completed his purchase of the diamonds. He wore the chamois-leather belt buckled tightly round his waist next to his inner shirt, and was able to defy the swell-mob, had those gentry been aware of the treasures which he carried about with him.

He wrote from Warwickshire to one of the best and most fashionable jewellers at the West End, and requested that a person who was thoroughly skilled in his business might be sent down to Maudesley Abbey, duly furnished with drawings of the newest designs in diamond necklaces, ear-rings, &c.

But when the jeweller's agent came, two or three days afterwards, Mr. Dunbar could find no design that suited him; and the man returned to London without having received an order, and without having even seen the brilliants which the banker had bought.

"Tell your employer that I will retain two or three of these designs," Mr. Dunbar said, selecting the drawings as he spoke; "and if, upon consideration, I find that one of them will suit me, I will communicate with your establishment. If not,

I shall take the diamonds to Paris, and get them made up there."

The jeweller ventured to suggest the inferiority of Parisian workmanship as compared with that of a first-rate English establishment; but Mr. Dunbar did not condescend to pay any attention to the young man's remonstrance.

"I shall write to your employer in due course," he said, coldly. "Good morning."

Major Vernon had returned to the Rose and Crown at Lisford. The deed which transferred to him the possession of Woodbine Cottage was speedily executed, and he took up his abode there. His establishment was composed of the old housekeeper, who had waited on the deceased admiral, and a young man-of-all-work, who was nephew to the housekeeper, and who had also been in the service of the late owner of the cottage.

From his new abode Mr. Vernon was able to keep a tolerably sharp look-out upon the two great houses in his neighbourhood—Maudesley Abbey and Jocelyn's Rock. Country people know every thing about their neighbours; and Mrs. Manders, the housekeeper, had means of communication with both "the Abbey" and "the Rock;" for she had a niece who was under-housemaid in the service of Henry Dunbar, and a grandson who was a helper in Sir Philip Jocelyn's stables. Nothing could have better pleased the new inhabitant of Woodbine Cottage, who was speedily on excellent terms with his housekeeper.

From her he heard that a jeweller's assistant had been to Maudesley, and had submitted a portfolio of designs to the millionaire.

"Which they do say," Mrs. Manders continued, "that Mr. Dunbar have laid out nigh upon half-a-million of money in diamonds; and that he is going to give his daughter, Lady Jocelyn, a set of jewels such as the Queen upon her throne never set eyes on. But Mr. Dunbar is rare and difficult to please, it seems; for the young man from the jeweller's, he says to Mrs. Grumbleton at the western lodge, he says, 'Your master is not easy to satisfy, ma'am,' he says; from which Mrs. Grumbleton gathers that he had not took a order from Mr. Dunbar."

Major Vernon whistled softly to himself when Mrs. Manders retired, after having imparted this piece of information.

"You're a clever fellow, dear friend," he muttered, as he lighted his cigar; "you're a stupendous fellow, dear boy; but your friend can see through less transparent blinds than this diamond business. It's well planned. It's neat, to say the least of it. And you've my best wishes, dear boy; but—you must pay for them—you must pay for them, Henry Dunbar."

This little conversation between the new tenant of Woodbine Cottage and his housekeeper occurred on the very evening on which Major Vernon took possession of his new abode. The next day was Sunday—a cold wintry Sunday; for the snow had been falling all through the last three days and nights, and lay deep on the ground, hiding the low thatched roofs, and making feathery festoons about the leafless branches, until Lisford looked like a village upon the top of a twelfth-cake. While the Sabbath-bells were ringing in the frosty atmosphere, Major Vernon opened the low white gate of his pleasant little garden, and went out upon the high road.

But not towards the church. Major Vernon was not going to church on this bright winter's morning. He went the other way, tramping through the snow, towards the eastern gates of Maudesley Park. He went in by a low iron gate, for there was a bridle-path through this part of the park—that very bridle-path by which Philip Jocelyn had ridden to Lisford so often in the autumn weather.

Major Vernon struck across this path, following the tracks of late footsteps in the deep snow, and thus took the nearest way to the Abbey. There he found all very quiet. The supercilious footman who admitted him to the hall seemed doubtful as to whether he should admit him any farther.

"Mr. Dunbar are hup," he said; "and have breakfasted, to the best of my knowledge, which the breakfast ekewpage have not yet been removed."

"So much the better," Major Vernon answered, coolly. "You may bring some fresh coffee, John; for I haven't made much of a breakfast myself; and if you'll tell the cook to devil the thigh of a turkey, with plenty of cayenne-pepper and a squeeze of lemon, I shall be obliged. You needn't trouble yourself; I know my way."

The Major opened the door leading to Mr. Dunbar's apartments, and walked without ceremony into the tapestried chamber, where he found the banker sitting near a table, upon which a silver coffee-service, a Dresden cup and saucer, and two or three covered dishes, gave evidence that Mr. Dunbar had been breakfasting.

Cold meats, raised pies, and other comestibles were laid out upon the carved-oak sideboard.

The Major paused upon the threshold of the chamber, and gravely contemplated his friend.

"It's comfortable!" he exclaimed; "to say the least of it, it's very comfortable, dear boy!"

The dear boy did not look particularly pleased as he lifted his eyes to his visitor's face.

"I thought you were in London?" he said.

"Which shows how very little you trouble yourself about the concerns of your neighbours," answered Major Vernon; "for if you had condescended to inquire about the movements of your humble friend, you would have been told that he had bought a comfortable little property in the neighbourhood, and settled down to do the respectable country gentleman for the remainder of his natural life—always supposing that the liberality of his honoured friend enables him to do the thing decently."

"Do you mean to say that you have bought property in this neighbourhood?"

"Yes; I am leasehold proprietor of Woodbine Cottage, near Lisford and Shorncliffe."

"And you mean to settle in Warwickshire?"

"I do."

Henry Dunbar smiled to himself as his friend said this.

"You're welcome to do so," he said, "as far as I'm concerned."

The Major looked at him sharply.

"Your sentiments are liberality itself, my dear friend. But I must respectfully remind you that the expenses attendant upon taking possession of my humble abode have been very heavy. In plain English, the two thou' which you so liberally advanced as the first instalment of future bounties, has melted like snow in a rapid thaw. I want another two thou', friend of my youth and patron of my later years. What's a thousand or so, more or less, to the senior partner in the house of D., D., and B.? Make it two five this time, and your petitioner will ever pray, &c. &c. &c. Make it two five, Prince of Maudesley!"

There is no need for me to record the interview between these two men. It was rather a long one; for, in congenial companionship, Major Vernon had plenty to say for himself: it was only when he felt himself out of his element and unappreciated that the Major wrapped himself in the dignity of silence, as in some mystic mantle, and retired for the time being from the outer world.

He did not leave Maudesley Abbey until he had succeeded in the object of his visit, and he carried away in his pocket-book cheques to the amount of two thousand five hundred pounds.

"I flatter myself I was just in the nick of time," the Major thought, as he walked back to Woodbine Cottage; "for, as sure as my name's what it is, my friend means a bolt. He means a bolt; and the money I've had to-day is the last I shall ever receive from that quarter."

Almost immediately after Major Vernon's departure, Henry Dunbar rang the bell for the servant who acted as his valet whenever he required the services of one, which was not often.

"I shall start for Paris to-night, Jeffreys," he said to this man. "I want to see what the French jewellers can do before I trust Lady Jocelyn's necklace into the hands of English workmen. I'm not well, and I want change of air and scene; so I shall start for Paris to-night. Pack a small portmanteau with every thing that's indispensable, but pack nothing unnecessary."

"Am I to go with you, sir?" the man asked.

Henry Dunbar looked at his watch, and seemed to reflect upon this question some moments before he answered.

"How do the up-trains go on a Sunday?" he asked.

"There's an express from the North stops at Rugby at six o'clock, sir. You might meet that, if you left Shorncliffe by the 4.35 train."

"I could do that," answered the banker; "it's only three o'clock. Pack my portmanteau at once, Jeffreys, and order the carriage to be ready for me at a quarter to four. No, I won't take you to Paris with me. You can follow me in a day or two with some more things."

"Yes, sir."

There was no such thing as bustle and confusion in a household organised like that of Mr. Dunbar. The valet packed his master's portmanteau and dressing-case; the carriage came round to the gravel-drive before the porch at the appointed moment; and five minutes afterwards Mr. Dunbar came out into the hall, with his greatcoat closely buttoned over his broad chest, and a leopard-skin travelling-rug flung across his shoulder.

Round his waist he wore the chamois-leather

belt which he had made with his own hands at the Clarendon Hotel. This belt had never quitted him since the night upon which he made it. The carriage conveyed him to the Shorncliffe station. He got out and went upon the platform. Although it was not yet five o'clock, the wintry light was fading in the gray sky, and in the railway station it was already dark. There were lamps here and there, but they only made separate splotches of light in the dusky atmosphere.

Henry Dunbar walked slowly up and down the platform. He was so deeply absorbed by his own thoughts that he was quite startled presently when a young man came close behind him, and addressed him eagerly.

"Mr. Dunbar," he said; "Mr. Dunbar!"

The banker turned sharply round, and recognised Arthur Lovell.

"Ah, my dear Lovell, is that you? You quite startled me."

"Are you going by the next train? I was so anxious to see you!"

"Why so?"

"Because there's some one here who very much wishes to see you; quite an old friend of yours, he says. Who do you think it is?"

"I don't know, I can't guess—I've so many old friends. I can't see any one, Lovell. I'm very ill. I saw a physician while I was in London; and he told me that my heart is diseased, and that if I wish to live, I must avoid any agitation, any sudden emotion, as I would avoid a deadly poison. Who is it that wants to see me?"

"Lord Herriston, the great Anglo-Indian statesman. He is a friend of my father's, and he has been very kind to me—indeed, he offered me an appointment, which I found it wisest to decline. He talked a great deal about you, when my father told him that you'd settled at Maudesley, and would have driven over to see you if he could have managed to spare the time, without losing his train. You'll see him, won't you?"

"Where is he?"

"Here, in the station—in the waiting-room.

He has been visiting in Warwickshire, and he lunched with my father *en passant;* he is going to Derby, and he's waiting for the down-train to take him on to the main line. You'll come and see him?"

"Yes, I shall be very glad; I—"

Henry Dunbar stopped suddenly, with his hand upon his side. The bell had been ringing while Lovell and the banker had stood upon the platform talking. The train came into the station at this moment.

"I shan't be able to see Lord Herriston to-night," Mr. Dunbar said, hurriedly; "I must go by this train, or I shall lose a day. Good-by, Lovell. Make my best compliments to Herriston; tell him I have been very ill. Good-by."

"Your portmanteau's in the carriage, sir," the servant said, pointing to the open door of a first-class compartment.

Henry Dunbar got into the carriage. At the moment of his doing so, an elderly gentleman came out of the waiting-room.

"Is this my train, Lovell?" he asked.

"No, my lord. Mr. Dunbar is here; he goes by this train. You'll have time to speak to him."

The train was moving. Lord Herriston was an active old fellow. He ran along the platform, looking into the carriages. But the old man's sight was not as good as his legs were; he looked eagerly into the carriage-windows, but he only saw a confusion of flickering lamplight, and strange faces, and newspapers unfurled in the hands of wakeful travellers, and the heads of sleepy passengers rolling and jolting against the padded sides of the carriage.

"My eyes are not what they used to be," he said, with a good-tempered laugh, when he went back to Arthur Lovell. "I didn't succeed in getting a glimpse of my old friend Henry Dunbar."

CHAPTER XIII.

STOPPED UPON THE WAY.

MR. DUNBAR leant back in the corner of his comfortable seat, with his eyes closed. But he was not asleep, he was only thinking; and every now and then he bent forward, and looked out of the window into the darkness of the night. He could only distinguish the faint outline of the landscape as the train swept on upon its way, past low meadows, where the snow lay white and stainless, unsullied by a passing footfall; and scanty patches of woodland, where the hardy firs looked black against the glittering whiteness of the ground.

The country was all so much alike under its thick shroud of snow, that Mr. Dunbar tried in vain to distinguish any landmarks upon the way.

The train by which he travelled stopped at every station; and, though the journey between

Shorncliffe and Rugby was only to last an hour, it seemed almost interminable to this impatient traveller, who was eager to stand upon the deck of one of Messrs. ——'s electric steamers, to feel the icy spray dashing into his face, and to see the town of Dover, shining like a flaming crescent against the darkness of the night, and the Calais lights in the distance rising up behind the black edge of the sea.

The banker looked at his watch, and made a calculation about the time. It was now a quarter past five; the train was to reach Rugby at ten minutes to six; at six the London express left Rugby; at a quarter to eight it reached London; at half-past eight the Dover mail would leave London-bridge station; and at half-past seven, or thereabouts, next morning, Henry Dunbar would be rattling through the streets of Paris.

And then? Was his journey to end in that brilliant city, or was he to go farther? That was a question whose answer was hidden in the traveller's own breast. He had not shown himself a communicative man at the best of times, and to-night he looked like a man whose soul is weighed down by the burden of a purpose which must be achieved at any cost of personal sacrifice.

He could not hear the names of the stations. He only heard those guttural and inarticulate sounds which railway officials roar out upon the darkness of the night, to the bewilderment of helpless travellers. His inability to distinguish the names of the stations annoyed him. The delay attendant upon every fresh stoppage worried him, as if the pause had been the weary interval of an hour. He sat with his watch in his hand; for every now and then he was seized with a sudden terror that the train had fallen out of its regular pace, and was crawling slowly along the rails.

What if it should not reach Rugby until after the London express had left the station?

Mr. Dunbar asked one of his fellow-travellers if this train was always punctual.

"Yes," the gentleman answered, coolly; "I believe it is generally pretty regular. But I don't know how the snow may affect the engine. There have been accidents in some parts of the country."

"In consequence of the depth of snow?"

"Yes. I understand so."

It was about ten minutes after this brief conversation, and within a quarter of an hour of the time at which the train was due at Rugby, when the carriage, which had rocked a good deal from the first, began to oscillate very violently. One meagre little elderly traveller turned rather pale, and looked nervously at his fellow-passengers; but the young man who had spoken to Henry Dunbar, and a bald-headed commercial-looking gentleman opposite to him, went on reading their newspapers as coolly as if the rocking of the carriage had been no more perilous than the lullaby motion of an infant's cradle, guided by a mother's gentle foot.

Mr. Dunbar never took his eyes from the dial of his watch. So the nervous traveller found no response to his look of terror.

He sat quietly for a minute or so, and then lowered the window near him, and let in a rush of icy wind, whereat the bald-headed commercial gentleman turned upon him rather fiercely, and asked him what he was about, and if he wanted to give them all inflammation of the lungs, by letting in an atmosphere that was two degrees below zéro. But the little elderly gentleman scarcely heard this remonstrance; his head was out of the window, and he was looking eagerly Rugby-wards along the line.

"I'm afraid there's something wrong," he said, drawing in his head for a moment, and looking with a scared white face at his fellow-passengers; "I'm really afraid there's something wrong. We're eight minutes behind our time, and I see the danger-signal up yonder, and the line seems blocked up with snow, and I really fear—"

He looked out again, and then drew in his head very suddenly.

"There's something coming!" he cried; "there's an engine coming—"

He never finished his sentence. There was a horrible smashing, tearing, grinding noise, that was louder than thunder, and more hideous than the crashing of cannon against the wooden walls of a brave ship.

That horrible sound was followed by a yell almost as horrible; and then there was nothing but death, and terror, and darkness, and anguish, and bewilderment; masses of shattered woodwork and iron heaped in direful confusion upon the blood-stained snow; human groans, stifled under the wrecks of shivered carriages; the cries of mothers whose children had been flung out of their arms into the very jaws of death; the piteous wail of children, who clung, warm and living, to the breasts of dead mothers, martyred in that moment of destruction; husbands parted from their wives; wives shrieking for their husbands; and, amidst all, brave men, with white faces, hurrying here and there, with lamps in their hands, half-maimed and wounded some of them, but forgetful of themselves in their care for the helpless wretches round them.

The express going northwards had run into the train from Shorncliffe, which had come upon the main line just nine minutes too late.

One by one the dead and wounded were carried away from the great heap of ruins; one by one the prostrate forms were borne away by quiet bearers, who did their duty calmly and fearlessly in that hideous scene of havoc and confusion. The great object to be achieved was the immediate clearance of the line; and the sound of pickaxes and shovels almost drowned those other dreadful sounds, the piteous moans of those sufferers who were so little hurt as to be conscious of their sufferings.

The train from Shorncliffe had been completely smashed. The northern express had suffered much less; but the engine-driver had been killed, and several of the passengers severely injured.

Henry Dunbar was amongst those who were carried away helpless and, to all appearance, lifeless from the ruin of the Shorncliffe train.

One of the banker's legs was broken, and he had received a blow upon the head, which had rendered him immediately unconscious.

But there were cases much worse than that of the banker; the surgeon who examined the sufferers said that Mr. Dunbar might recover from his injuries in two or three months, if he was carefully treated. The fracture of the leg was very simple; and if the limb was skilfully set, there would not be the least fear of contraction.

Half-a-dozen surgeons were busy in one of the waiting-rooms at the Rugby station, whither the sufferers had been conveyed, and one of them took possession of the banker.

Mr. Dunbar's card-case had been found in the breast-pocket of his overcoat, and a great many people in the waiting-room knew that the gentleman with the white face and gray moustache, lying so quietly upon one of the broad sofas, was no less a personage than Henry Dunbar, of Maudesley Abbey and St. Gundolph Lane. The surgeon knew it, and thought his good angel had sent this particular patient across his pathway.

He made immediate arrangements for bearing off Mr. Dunbar to the nearest hotel; he sent for his assistant; and in a quarter of an hour's time the millionaire was restored to consciousness, and opened his eyes upon the eager faces of two medical gentlemen, and upon a room that was strange to him.

The banker looked about him with an expression of perplexity, and then asked where he was. He knew nothing of the accident itself, and he had quite lost the recollection of all that had occurred immediately before the accident, or, indeed, from the time of his leaving Maudesley Abbey.

It was only little by little that the memory of the events of that day returned to him. He had wanted to leave Maudesley; he had wanted to go abroad—to go upon a journey that was no new purpose in his mind. Had he actually set out upon that journey? Yes, surely, he must have started upon it; but what had happened, then?

He asked the surgeon what had happened, and why it was that he found himself in that strange place.

Mr. Daphney, the Rugby surgeon, told his patient all about the accident, in such a bland, pleasant way, that any body might have thought the collision of a couple of engines rather an agreeable little episode in a man's life.

"But we are doing admirably, sir," Mr. Daphney concluded; "nothing could be more desirable than the way in which we are going on; and when our leg has been set, and we've taken a cooling draught, we shall be quite comfortable for the night. I really never saw a cleaner fracture —never, I can assure you."

But Mr. Dunbar raised himself into a sitting position, in spite of the remonstrances of his medical attendant, and looked anxiously about him.

"You say this place is Rugby?" he asked, moodily.

"Yes, this is Rugby," answered the surgeon, smiling, and rubbing his hands, almost as if he would have said, "Now isn't *that* delightful?" "Yes, this is the Queen's Hotel, Rugby; and I'm sure that every attention which the proprietor, Mr. ——"

"I must get away from this place to-night," said Mr. Dunbar, interrupting the surgeon rather unceremoniously.

"To-night, my dear sir!" cried Mr. Daphney; "impossible—utterly impossible—suicide on your part, my dear sir, if you attempted it, and murder upon mine, if I allowed you to carry out such an idea. You will be a prisoner here for a month or so, sir, I regret to say; but we shall do all in our power to make your sojourn agreeable."

The surgeon could not help looking cheerful as he made this announcement; but seeing a very black and ominous expression upon the face of his patient, he contrived to modify the radiance of his own countenance.

"Our first proceeding, sir, must be to straighten this poor leg," he said, soothingly. "We shall place the leg in a cradle, from the thigh downwards: but I won't trouble you with technical details. I doubt if we shall be justified in setting the leg to-night; we must reduce the swelling before we can venture upon any important step. A cooling lotion, applied with linen cloths, must be kept on all night. I have made arrangements for a nurse, and my assistant will also remain here all night to supervise her movements."

The banker groaned aloud.

"I want to get to London," he said. "I must get to London!"

The surgeon and his assistant removed Mr. Dunbar's clothes. His trousers had to be cut away from his broken leg before any thing could be done. Mr. Daphney removed his patient's coat and waistcoat; but the linen shirt was left, and the chamois-leather belt worn by the banker was under this shirt, next to and over a waistcoat of scarlet flannel.

"I wear a leather belt next my flannel waistcoat," Mr. Dunbar said, as the two men were undressing him; "I don't wish it to be removed."

He fainted away presently, for his leg was very painful; and on reviving from his fainting fit, he looked very suspiciously at his attendants, and put his hand to the buckle of his belt, in order to make himself sure that it had not been tampered with.

All through the long, feverish, restless night he lay pondering over this miserable interruption of his journey, while the sick-nurse and the surgeon's assistant alternately slopped cooling lotions about his wretched broken leg.

"To think that *this* should happen," he muttered to himself every now and then. "Amongst all the things I've ever dreaded, I never thought of this."

His leg was set in the course of the next day, and in the evening he had a long conversation with the surgeon.

This time Henry Dunbar did not speak so much of his anxiety to get away upon the second stage of his continental journey. His servant Jeffreys arrived at Rugby in the course of the day; for the news of the accident had reached Maudesley Abbey, and it was known that Mr. Dunbar had been a sufferer.

To-night Henry Dunbar only spoke of the misery of being in a strange house.

"I want to get back to Maudesley," he said. "If you can manage to take me there, Mr. Daphney, and look after me until I've got over the effects of this accident, I shall be very happy to make you any compensation you please for whatever loss your absence from Rugby might entail upon you."

This was a very diplomatic speech; Mr. Dunbar knew that the surgeon would not care to let so rich a patient out of his hands; but he fancied that Mr. Daphney would have no objection to carrying his patient in triumph to Maudesley Abbey, to the admiration of the unprofessional public, and to the aggravation of rival medical men.

He was not mistaken in his estimate of human nature. At the end of the week he had succeeded in persuading the surgeon to agree to his removal, and upon the second Monday after the railway accident, Henry Dunbar was placed in a compartment which was specially prepared for him in the Shorncliffe train, and was conveyed from Shorncliffe station to Maudesley Abbey, without undergoing any change of position upon the road, and very carefully tended throughout the journey by Mr. Daphney and Jeffreys the valet.

They wheeled Mr. Dunbar's bed into his favourite tapestried chamber, and laid him there, to drag out long dreary days and nights, waiting till his broken bones should unite, and he should be free to go whither he pleased. He was not a very patient sufferer; he bore the pain well enough, but he chafed perpetually against the delay; and every morning he asked the surgeon the same question—

"When shall I be strong enough to walk about?"

CHAPTER XIV.

CLEMENT AUSTIN MAKES A SACRIFICE.

MARGARET WILMOT had promised to become the wife of the man she loved; but she had given that promise very reluctantly, and only upon one condition. The condition was that, before her marriage with Clement Austin took place, the mystery of her father's death should be cleared up for ever.

"I cannot be your wife so long as the secret of that cruel deed remains unknown," she said to Clement. "It seems to me as if I have been already wickedly neglectful of a solemn duty. Who had my father to love him and remember him in all the world but me? and who should avenge his death if I do not? He was an outcast from society; and people think it a very small thing that, after having led a reckless life, he should die a cruel death. If Henry Dunbar, the rich banker, had been murdered, the police would never have rested until the assassin had been discovered. But who cares what became of Joseph Wilmot, except his daughter? His death makes no blank in the world: except to me—except to me!"

Clement Austin did not forget his promise to do his uttermost towards the discovery of the banker's guilt. He believed that Henry Dunbar was the murderer of his old servant; and he had believed it ever since that day upon which the banker stole, like a detected thief, out of the house in St. Gundolph Lane.

It was just possible that Henry Dunbar might avoid Joseph Wilmot's daughter from a natural horror of the events connected with his return to England: but that the banker should resort to a cowardly stratagem to escape from an interview with the girl could scarcely be accounted for, except by the fact of his guilt.

He had an insurmountable terror of seeing this girl, because he was the murderer of her father.

The longer Clement Austin deliberated upon this business, the more certainly he came to that one terrible conclusion: Henry Dunbar was guilty. He would gladly have thought otherwise: and he would have been very happy had he been able to tell Margaret Wilmot that the mystery of her father's death was a mystery that would never be solved upon this earth: but he could not do so; he could only bow his head before the awful necessity that urged him on to take his part in this drama of crime—the part of an avenger.

But a cashier in a London bank has very little time to play any part in life's history, except that quiet *rôle* which seems chiefly to consist in locking and unlocking iron safes, peering furtively into mysterious ledgers, and shovelling about new sovereigns as coolly as if they were Wallsend or Clay-Cross coals.

Clement Austin's life was not an easy one, and he had no time to turn amateur detective, even in the service of the woman he loved.

He had no time to turn amateur detective so

long as he remained at the banking-house in St. Gundolph Lane.

But could he remain there? That question arose in his mind, and took a very serious form. Was it possible to remain in that house when he believed the principal member of it to be one of the most infamous of men?

No; it was quite impossible for him to remain in his present situation. So long as he took a salary from Dunbar, Dunbar, and Balderby, he was in a manner under obligation to Henry Dunbar. He could not remain in this man's service, and yet at the same time play the spy upon his actions, and work heart and soul to drag the dreadful secret of his life into the light of day.

Thus it was that towards the close of the week in which Henry Dunbar, for the first time after his return from India, visited the banking-offices, Clement Austin handed a formal notice of resignation to Mr. Balderby. The cashier could not immediately resign his situation, but was compelled to give his employers a month's notice of the withdrawal of his services.

A thunderbolt falling upon the morocco-covered writing-table in Mr. Balderby's private parlour could scarcely have been more astonishing to the junior partner than this letter which Clement Austin handed him very quietly and very respectfully.

There were many reasons why Clement Austin should remain in the banking-house. His father had lived for thirty years, and had eventually died, in the employment of Dunbar and Dunbar. He had been a great favourite with the brothers; and Clement had been admitted into the house as a boy, and had received much notice from Percival. More than this, he had every chance of being admitted ere long to a junior partnership upon very easy terms, which junior partnership would of course be the high road to a great fortune.

Mr. Balderby sat with the letter open in his hands, staring at the lines before him as if he was scarcely able to comprehend their purport.

"Do you *mean* this, Austin?" he said at last.

"Yes, sir. Circumstances over which I have no control compel me to offer you my resignation."

"Have you quarrelled with any body in the office? Has any thing occurred in the house that has made you uncomfortable?"

"No, indeed, Mr. Balderby; I am very comfortable in my position."

The junior partner leaned back in his chair, and stared at the cashier as if he had been trying to detect the traces of incipient insanity in the young man's countenance.

"You are comfortable in your position, and yet you— Oh! I suppose the real truth of the matter is, that you have heard of something better, and you are ready to give us the go-by, in order to improve your own circumstances?" said Mr. Balderby, with a tone of pique; "though I really don't see how you can very well be better off any where than you are here," he added, thoughtfully.

"You do me wrong, sir, when you think that I could willingly leave you for my own advantage," Clement answered, quietly. "I have no better engagement, nor have I even a prospect of any engagement."

"You haven't!" exclaimed the junior partner; "and yet you throw away such a chance as only falls to the lot of one man in a thousand! I don't particularly care about guessing riddles, Mr. Austin; perhaps you'll be kind enough to tell me frankly why you want to leave us?"

"I regret to say that it is impossible for me to do so, sir," replied the cashier; "my motive for leaving this house, which is a kind of second home to me, is no frivolous one, believe me. I have weighed well the step I am about to take, and I am quite aware that I sacrifice very excellent prospects in throwing up my present situation. But the reason of my resignation must remain a secret; for the present at least. If ever the day comes when I am able to explain my conduct, I believe that you will give me your hand, and say to me, 'Clement Austin, you only did your duty.'"

"Clement," said Mr. Balderby, "you are an excellent fellow; but you certainly must have got some romantic crotchet in your head, or you could never have thought of writing such a letter as this. Are you going to be married? Is that your reason for leaving us? Have you fascinated some wealthy heiress, and are you going to retire into splendid slavery?"

"No, sir. I am engaged to be married; but the lady whom I hope to call my wife is poor, and I have every necessity to be a working man for the rest of my life."

"Well, then, my dear fellow, it's a riddle; and, as I said before, I'm not good at guessing enigmas. There, my boy; go home and sleep upon this; and come back to me to-morrow morning, and tell me to throw this stupid letter in the fire—that's the wisest thing you can do. Good night."

But, in spite of all that Mr. Balderby could say, Clement Austin steadily adhered to his resolution. He worked early and late during the month in which he remained at his post, preparing the ledgers, balancing accounts, and making things straight and easy for the new cashier. He told Margaret Wilmot of what he had done; but he did not tell her the extent of the sacrifice which he had made for her sake. She was the only person who knew the real motive of his conduct; for to his mother he said very little more than he had said to Mr. Balderby.

"I shall be able to tell you my motives for leaving the banking-house at some future time, dear mother," he said; "until that time I can only entreat you to trust me, and to believe that I have acted for the best."

"I do believe it, my dear," answered the widow, cheerfully; "when did you ever do any thing that wasn't wise and good?"

Her only son, Clement was the god of this simple woman's idolatry; and if he had seen fit to turn her out of doors, and ask her to beg by his side in the streets of the city, I doubt if she would not have imagined some hidden wisdom lurking at the bottom of his apparently irrational proceedings. So she made no objection to his abandoning his desk in the house of Dunbar, Dunbar, and Balderby.

"We shall be poorer, I suppose, Clem," Mrs. Austin said; "but that's very little consequence; for your dear father left me so comfortably off that I can very well afford to keep house for my only son; and I shall have you more at home, dear, and that will indeed be happiness."

But Clement told his mother that he had some very important business on hand just then, which would occupy him a good deal; and indeed the first step necessary would be a journey to Shorncliffe, in Warwickshire.

"Why, that's where you went to school, Clem!"

"Yes, mother."

"And it's near Mr. Percival Dunbar—or, at least, Mr. Henry Dunbar's country house."

"Yes, mother," answered Clement. "Now the business in which I am engaged is—is rather of a difficult nature, and I want legal help. My old schoolfellow Arthur Lovell, who is as good a fellow as ever breathed, has been educated for the law, and is now a solicitor. He lives at Shorncliffe with his father John Lovell, who is also a solicitor, and a man of some standing in the county. I shall run down to Shorncliffe, see my old friend, and get his advice; and if you'll bring Margaret down for a few days' change of air, we'll stop at the dear old Reindeer, where you used to come, mother, when I was at school, and where you used to give me such jolly dinners in the days when a good dinner was a treat to a hungry schoolboy."

Mrs. Austin smiled at her son; she smiled tenderly as she remembered his bright boyhood. Mothers with only sons are not very strong-minded. Had Clement proposed a trip to the moon, she would scarcely have known how to refuse him her company on the expedition.

She shivered a little, and looked rather doubtfully from the blazing fire which lit up the cosy drawing-room to the cold gray sky outside the window.

"The beginning of January isn't the pleasantest time in all the year for a trip into the country, Clem dear," she said; "but I should certainly be very lonely at home without you. And as to poor Madge, of course it would be a great treat to her to get away from her pupils, and have a peep at the genuine country, even though there isn't a single leaf upon the trees. So I suppose I must say yes. But do tell me all about this business, there's a dear good boy."

Unfortunately the dear good boy was obliged to tell his mother that the business in question was, like his motive for resigning his situation, a profound secret, and that it must remain so for some time to come.

"Wait, dear mother," he said; "you shall know all about it by and by. Believe me, when I tell you that it's not a very pleasant business," he added, with a sigh.

"It's not unpleasant for you, I hope, Clement?"

"It isn't pleasant for any one who is concerned in it, mother," answered the young man, thoughtfully; "it's altogether a miserable business; but I'm not concerned in it as a principal, you know, dear mother; and when it's all over we shall only look back upon it as the passing of a black cloud over our lives, and you will say that I have done my duty. Dearest mother, don't look so puzzled," added Clement; "this matter *must* remain a secret for the present. Only wait, and trust me."

"I will, my dear boy," Mrs. Austin said, presently. "I will trust you with all my heart; for I know how good you are. But I don't like secrets, Clem; secrets always make me uncomfortable."

No more was said upon this subject, and it was arranged by and by that Mrs. Austin and Margaret should prepare to start for Warwickshire at the beginning of the following week, when Clement would be freed from all engagements to Messrs. Dunbar, Dunbar, and Balderby.

Margaret had waited very patiently for this time, in which Clement would be free to give her all his help in that awful task which lay before her—the discovery of Henry Dunbar's guilt.

"You will go to Shorncliffe with my mother," Clement Austin said, upon the evening after his conversation with the widow; "you will go with her, Madge, ostensibly upon a little pleasure-trip. Once there, we shall be able to contrive an interview with Mr. Dunbar. He is a prisoner at Maudesley Abbey, laid up by the effect of his accident the other day, but not too ill to see people, Balderby says; therefore I should think we may be able to plan an interview between you and him. You still hold to your original purpose? You still wish to *see* Henry Dunbar?"

"Yes," answered Margaret, thoughtfully; "I want to see him. I want to look straight into the face of the man whom I believe to be my father's murderer. I don't know why it is, but this purpose has been uppermost in my mind ever since I heard of that dreadful journey to Winchester; ever since I first knew that my father had been murdered while travelling with Henry Dunbar. It might, as you have said, be wiser to watch and wait, and to avoid all chance of alarming this man. But I can't be wise. I want to see him. I want to look in his face, and see if his eyes can meet mine."

"You shall see him then, dear girl. A woman's instinct is sometimes worth more than a man's wisdom. You shall see Henry Dunbar. I know that my old schoolfellow Arthur Lovell will help me, with all his heart and soul. I have called again upon the Scotland-Yard people, and I gave them a minute description of the scene in St. Gundolph Lane; but they only shrugged their shoulders, and said the circumstances looked queer, but were not strong enough to act upon. If any body can help us, Arthur Lovell can; for he was present at the inquest and all further examination of the witnesses at Winchester."

If Margaret Wilmot and Clement Austin had been going upon any other errand than that which took them to Warwickshire, the journey to Shorncliffe might have been very pleasant to them.

To Margaret, this comfortable journey in the cushioned corner of a first-class carriage, respectfully waited upon by the man she loved, possessed at least the charm of novelty. Her journeys hitherto had been long wearisome pilgrimages in draughty third-class carriages, with noisy company, and in an atmosphere pervaded by a powerful effluvium of various kinds of alcohol.

Her life had been a very hard one, darkened by the ever-brooding shadow of disgrace. It was new to her to sit quietly looking out at the low meadows and glimmering white-walled villas, the patches of sparse woodland, the distant villages, the glimpses of rippling water, shining in the wintry sun. It was new to her to be loved by people whose minds were unembittered by the baneful memories of wrong and crime. It was new to her to hear gentle voices, sweet Christian-like words; it was new to her to breathe the bright atmosphere that surrounds those who lead a virtuous, God-fearing life.

But there is little sunshine without its attendant shadow. The shadow upon Margaret's life now was the shadow of that coming task—that horrible work which must be done—before she could be free to thank God for His mercies, and to be happy.

The London train reached Shorncliffe early in the afternoon. Clement Austin hired a roomy old fly, and carried off his companions to the Reindeer.

The Reindeer was a comfortable old-fashioned hotel. It had been a very grand place in the coaching days, and you entered the hostelry by a broad and ponderous archway, under which High-flyers and Electrics had driven triumphantly in the days that were for ever gone.

The house was a roomy old place, with long corridors and wide staircases; noble staircases, with broad, slippery, oaken banisters and shallow steps. The rooms were grand and big, with bow-windows so spotless in their cleanliness that they had rather a cold effect upon a January day, and were apt to inspire in the vulgar mind the fancy that a little dirt or smoke would look warmer and more comfortable. Certainly, if the Reindeer had a fault, it was that it was too clean. Every thing was actually slippery with cleanliness, from the newly-calendered chintz that covered the sofa and the chair-cushions, to the copper coal-scuttle that glittered by the side of the dazzling brass fender. There were faint odours of soft soap in the bedchambers, which no amount of dried lavender could overcome. There was an effluvium of vitriol about all the brass-work, and there was a good deal of brass-work in the Reindeer: and if one species of decoration is more conducive to shivering than another, it certainly is brass-work in a state of high polish.

There was no dish ever devised by mortal cook which the sojourner at the Reindeer could not have, according to the preliminary statement of the landlord: but with whatever ambitious design the sojourner began to talk about dinner, it always ended, somehow or other, by his ordering a chicken, a little bit of boiled bacon, a dish of cutlets, and a tart. There were days upon which divers species of fish were to be had in Shorncliffe: but the sojourner at the Reindeer rarely happened to hit upon one of those days.

Clement Austin installed Margaret and the widow in a sitting-room which would have comfortably accommodated about forty people. There was a bow-window quite large enough for the requirements of a small family, and Mrs. Austin settled herself there, while the landlord was struggling with a refractory fire, and pretending not to know that the grate was damp.

Clement went through the usual fiction of deliberation as to what he should have for dinner, and of course ended with the perennial chicken and cutlets.

"I haven't the fine appetite I had fifteen years ago, Mr. Gilwood," he said to the landlord, "when my mother yonder, who hasn't grown fifteen days older in all those fifteen years,—bless her dear motherly heart!—used to come down to see me at the academy in the Lisford Road, and give me a dinner in this dear old room. I thought your cutlets the most ethereal morsels ever dished by mortal cook, Mr. Gilwood, and this room the best place in all the world. You know Mr. Lovell, Mr. Arthur Lovell?"

"Yes, sir; and a very nice young gentleman he is."

"He's settled in Shorncliffe, I suppose?"

"Well, I believe he is, sir. There was some talk of his going out to India, in a Government appointment, sir, or something of that sort; but

I'm given to understand that it's all off now, and that Mr. Arthur is to go into partnership with his father; and a very clever young lawyer he is, I've been told."

"So much the better," answered Clement, "for I want to consult him upon a little matter of business. Good by, mother! Take care of Madge, and make yourselves as comfortable as you can. I think the fire will burn now, Mr. Gilwood. I shan't be away above an hour, I daresay; and then I'll come and take you for a walk before dinner. God bless you, my poor Madge!" Clement whispered, as Margaret followed him to the door of the room, and looked wistfully after him as he went down the staircase.

Mrs. Austin had once cherished ambitious views with regard to her son's matrimonial prospects; but she had freely given them up when she found that he had set his heart upon winning Margaret Wilmot for his wife. The good mother had made this sacrifice willingly and without complaint, as she would have made any other sacrifice for her dearly-beloved only son; and she found the reward of her devotion; for Margaret, this penniless, friendless girl, had become very dear to her—a real daughter, not in law, but bound by the sweet ties of gratitude and affection.

"And I was such a silly old creature, my dear," the widow said to Margaret, as they sat in the bow-window looking out into the quiet street; "I was so worldly-minded that I wanted Clement to marry a rich woman, so that I might have some stuck-up daughter-in-law, who would despise her husband's mother, and estrange my boy from me, and make my old age miserable. That's what I wanted, Madge, and what I might have had, perhaps, if Clem hadn't been wiser than his silly old mother. And, thanks to him, I've got the sweetest, truest, brightest girl that ever lived; though you're not as bright as usual to-day, Madge," Mrs. Austin added, thoughtfully. "You haven't smiled once this morning, my dear, and you seem as if you'd something on your mind."

"I've been thinking of my poor father," Margaret answered, quietly.

"To be sure, my dear; and I might have

known as much, my poor tender-hearted lamb. I know how unhappy those thoughts always make you."

Clement Austin had not been at Shorncliffe for three years. He had visited Maudesley Abbey several times during the lifetime of Percival Dunbar, for he had been a favourite with the old man; and he had been four years at a boarding-school kept by a clergyman of the Church of England in a fine old brick mansion on the Lisford Road.

The town of Shorncliffe was therefore familiar to Mr. Austin; and he looked neither to the right nor to the left as he walked towards the archway of St. Gwendoline's church, near which Mr. Lovell's house was situated.

He found Arthur at home, and very delighted to see his old schoolfellow. The two young men went into a little panelled room, looking into the garden, a cosy little room which Arthur Lovell called his study; and here they sat together for upwards of an hour, discussing the circumstances of the murder at Winchester, and the conduct of Mr. Dunbar since that event.

In the course of that interview, Clement Austin plainly perceived that Arthur Lovell had come to the same conclusion as himself, though the young lawyer was slow to express his opinion.

"I cannot bear to think it," he said; "I know Laura Dunbar,—that is to say, Lady Jocelyn,—and it is too horrible to me to imagine that her father is guilty of this crime. What would be that innocent girl's feelings if it should be so, and if her father's guilt should be brought home to him!"

"Yes, it would be very terrible for Lady Jocelyn, no doubt," Clement answered; "but that consideration must not hinder the course of justice. I think this man's position has served him as a shield from the very first. People have thought it next to impossible that Henry Dunbar could be guilty of a crime, while they would have been ready enough to suspect some penniless vagabond of any iniquity."

Arthur Lovell told Clement that the banker was still at Maudesley, bound a prisoner by his broken leg, which was going on favourably enough, but very slowly.

Mr. Dunbar had expressed a wish to go abroad, in spite of his broken leg, and had only desisted from his design of being conveyed somehow or other from place to place, when he was told that any such imprudence might result in permanent lameness.

"Keep yourself quiet, and submit to the necessities of your accident, and you'll recover quickly," the surgeon told his patient. "Try to hurry the work of nature, and you'll have cause to repent your impatience for the remainder of your life."

So Henry Dunbar had been obliged to submit himself to the decrees of Fate, and to lie day after day, and night after night, upon his bed in the tapestried chamber, staring at the fire, or the figure of his valet and attendant, nodding in the easy-chair by the hearth; or listening to the cinders falling from the grate, and the moaning of the winter wind amongst the bare branches of the elms.

The banker was getting better and stronger every day, Arthur Lovell said. His attendants were able to remove him from one chamber to another; a pair of crutches had been made for him, but he had not yet been able to make his first feeble trial of them. He was fain to content himself with being carried to an easy-chair, to sit for a few hours, wrapped in blankets, with the leopard-skin rug about his legs. No man could have been more completely a prisoner than this man had become by the result of the fatal accident near Rugby.

"Providence has thrown him into my power," Margaret said, when Clement repeated to her the information which he had received from Arthur Lovell,—"Providence has thrown this man into my power; for he can no longer escape, and, surrounded by his own servants, he will scarcely dare to refuse to see me; he will surely never be so unwise as to betray his terror of me."

"And if he does refuse——"

"If he does, I will invent some stratagem by which I may see him. But he will not refuse.

When he finds that I am so resolute as to follow him here, he will not refuse to see me."

This conversation took place during a brief walk which the lovers took in the wintry dusk, while Mrs. Austin nodded by the fire in that comfortable half-hour which precedes dinner.

CHAPTER XV.

WHAT HAPPENED AT MAUDESLEY ABBEY.

EARLY the next day Clement Austin walked to Maudesley Abbey, in order to procure all the information likely to facilitate Margaret Wilmot's grand purpose. He stopped at the gate of the principal lodge. The woman who kept it was an old servant of the Dunbar family, and had known Clement Austin in Percival Dunbar's lifetime. She gave him a hearty welcome, and he had no difficulty whatever in setting her tongue in motion upon the subject of Henry Dunbar.

She told him a great deal; she told him that the present owner of the Abbey never had been liked, and never would be liked: for his stern and gloomy manner was so unlike his father's easy, affable good nature, that people were always drawing comparisons between the dead man and the living.

This, in a few words, is the substance of what the worthy woman said in a good many words. Mrs. Grumbleton gave Clement all the information he required as to the banker's daily movements at the present time. Henry Dunbar was now in the habit of rising about two o'clock in the day, at which time he was assisted from his bedroom to his sitting-room, where he remained until seven or eight o'clock in the evening. He had no visitors, except the surgeon Mr. Daphney, who lived in the Abbey, and a gentleman called Vernon, who had bought Woodbine Cottage, near Lisford, and who now and then was admitted to Mr. Dunbar's sitting-room.

This was all Clement Austin wanted to know. Surely it might be possible, with a little clever management, to throw the banker completely off his guard, and to bring about the long-delayed interview between him and Margaret Wilmot.

Clement returned to the Reindeer, had a brief conversation with Margaret, and made all arrangements.

At four o'clock that afternoon, Miss Wilmot

and her lover left the Reindeer in a fly; at a quarter to five the fly stopped at the lodge-gates.

"I will walk to the house," Margaret said; "my coming will attract less notice. But I may be detained for some time, Clement. Pray, don't wait for me. Your dear mother will be alarmed if you are very long absent. Go back to her, and send the fly for me by and by."

"Nonsense, Madge. I shall wait for you, however long you may be. Do you think my heart is not as much engaged in any thing that may influence your fate as even your own can be? I won't go with you to the Abbey; for it will be as well that Henry Dunbar should remain in ignorance of my presence in the neighbourhood. I will walk up and down the road here, and wait for you."

"But you may have to wait so long, Clement."

"No matter how long. I can wait patiently, but I could not endure to go home and leave you, Madge."

They were standing before the great iron gates as Clement said this. He pressed Margaret's cold hand; he could feel how cold it was, even through her glove; and then rang the bell. She looked at him as the gate was opened; she turned and looked at him with a strangely earnest gaze as she crossed the boundary of Henry Dunbar's domain, and then walked slowly along the broad avenue.

That last look had shown Clement Austin a pale resolute face, something like the countenance of a fair young martyr going quietly to the stake.

He walked away from the gates, and they shut behind him with a loud clanging noise. Then he went back to them, and watched Margaret's figure growing dim and distant in the gathering dusk as she approached the Abbey. A faint glow of crimson firelight reddened the gravel-drive before the windows of Mr. Dunbar's apartments, and there was a footman airing himself under the shadow of the porch, with a glimmer of light shining out of the hall behind him.

"I do not suppose I shall have to wait very long for my poor girl," Clement thought, as he left the gates, and walked briskly up and down the road. "Henry Dunbar is a resolute man; he will refuse to see her to-day, as he refused before."

Margaret found the footman lolling against the clustered pillars of the gothic porch, staring thoughtfully at the low evening light, yellow and red behind the brown trunks of the elms, and picking his teeth with a gold toothpick.

The sight of the open hall-door, and this languid footman lolling in the porch, suddenly inspired Margaret Wilmot with a new idea. Would it not be possible to slip quietly past this man, and walk straight to the apartments of Mr. Dunbar, unquestioned, uninterrupted?

Clement had pointed out to her the windows of the rooms occupied by the banker. They were on the left-hand side of the entrance-hall. It would be impossible for her to mistake the door leading to them. It was dusk, and she was very plainly dressed, with a black-straw bonnet, and a veil over her face. Surely she might deceive this languid footman by affecting to be some hanger-on of the household, which of course was a large one.

In that case she had no right to present herself at the front-door, certainly; but then, before the languid footman could recover from the first shock of indignation at her impertinence, she might slip past him, and reach the door leading to those apartments in which the banker hid himself and his guilt.

Margaret lingered a little in the avenue, watching for a favourable opportunity in which she might hazard this attempt. She waited five minutes or so.

The curve of the avenue screened her, in some wise, from the man in the porch, who never happened to roll his languid eyes towards the spot where she was standing.

A flight of rooks came scudding through the sky presently, very much excited, and cawing and screeching as if they had been an ornithological fire-brigade hurrying to extinguish the flames of some distant rookery.

The footman, who was suffering acutely from the complaint of not knowing what to do with himself, came out of the porch and stood in the middle of the gravelled drive, with his back towards Margaret, staring at the birds as they flew westward.

This was her opportunity. The girl hurried to the door with a light step; so light upon the smooth solid gravel that the footman heard nothing until she was on the broad stone step under the porch, when the fluttering of her skirt, as it brushed against the pillars, roused him from a species of trance or reverie.

He turned sharply round, as upon a pivot, and stared aghast at the retreating figure under the porch.

"Hi, you there, young woman!" he exclaimed, without stirring from his post; "where are you going to? What's the meaning of your coming to this door? Are you aware that there's such a place as a servants' 'all and a servants' hentrance?"

But the languid retainer was too late. Margaret's hand was upon the massive knob of the door on the left of the hall before the footman had put this last indignant question.

He listened for an apologetic murmur from

the young woman; but, hearing none, concluded that she had found her way to the servants' hall, where she had most likely some business or other with one of the female members of the household.

"A dressmaker, I dessay," the footman thought. "Those gals spend all their earnings in finery and fallalls, instead of behaving like respectable young women, and saving up their money against they can go into the public line with a man of their chice."

He yawned, and went on staring at the rooks, without troubling himself any further about the impertinent young person who had dared to present herself at the grand entrance.

Margaret opened the door, and went into the room next the hall.

It was a handsome apartment, lined with books from the floor to the ceiling; but it was quite empty, and there was no fire burning in the grate. The girl put up her veil, and looked about her. She was very, very pale now, and trembled violently; but she controlled her agitation by a great effort, and went slowly on to the next room.

The second room was empty like the first; but the door between it and the next chamber was wide open, and Margaret saw the firelight shining upon the faded tapestry, and reflected in the sombre depths of the polished oak-furniture. She heard the low sound of the light ashes falling on the hearth, and the snorting breath of a dog.

She knew that the man she sought, and had so long sought without avail, was in that room. Alone; for there was no murmur of voices, no sound of any one moving in the apartment. That hour, to which Margaret Wilmot had looked as the great crisis of her life, had come; and her courage failed her all at once, and her heart sank in her breast on the very threshold of the chamber in which she was to stand face to face with Henry Dunbar.

"The murderer of my father!" she thought; "the man whose influence blighted my father's life, and made him what he was. The man, through whose reckless sin my father lived a life that left him, oh! how sadly unprepared to die! The man who, knowing this, sent his victim before an offended God, without so much warning as would have given him time to think one prayer. I am going to meet *that* man face to face!"

Her breath came in faint gasps, and the firelit chamber swam before her eyes as she crossed the threshold of that door, and went into the room where Henry Dunbar was sitting alone before the low fire.

He was wrapped in crimson draperies of thick woollen stuff, and the leopard-skin railway rug was muffled about his knees. A dog of the bull-dog breed was lying asleep at the banker's feet, half-hidden in the folds of the leopard-skin. Henry Dunbar's head was bent over the fire, and his eyes were closed in a kind of dozing sleep, as Margaret Wilmot went into the room.

There was an empty chair opposite to that in which the banker sat; an old-fashioned, carved oak-chair, with a high back and crimson-morocco cushions. Margaret went softly up to this chair, and laid her hand upon the oaken framework. Her footsteps made no sound on the thick Turkey carpet; the banker never stirred from his doze, and even the dog at his feet slept on.

"Mr. Dunbar!" cried Margaret, in a clear, resolute voice; "awake! it is I, Margaret Wilmot, the daughter of the man who was murdered in the grove near Winchester!"

The dog awoke, and snapped at her. The man lifted his head, and looked at her. Even the fire seemed roused by the sound of her voice; for a little jet of vivid light leapt up out of the smouldering log, and lighted the scared face of the banker.

Clement Austin had promised Margaret to wait for her, and to wait patiently; and he meant to keep his promise. But there are some limits even to the patience of a lover, though he were the veriest knight-errant who was ever eager to shiver a lance or hack the edge of a battle-axe for love of his liege lady. When you have nothing to do but to walk up and down a few yards of hard dusty high road, upon a bleak evening in January, an hour more or less is of considerable consequence. Five o'clock struck about ten minutes after Margaret Wilmot had entered the park, and Clement thought to himself that even if Margaret were successful in obtaining an interview with the banker, that interview would be over before six. But the faint strokes of Lisford-church clock died away upon the cold evening wind, and Clement was still pacing up and down, and the fly was still waiting; the horse comfortable enough with a rug upon his back and his nose in a bag of oats; the man walking up and down by the side of the vehicle, slapping his gloved hands across his shoulders every now and then to keep himself warm. In that long hour between six and seven, Clement Austin's patience wore itself almost threadbare. It is one thing to ride into the lists on a prancing steed, caparisoned with embroidered trappings, worked by the fair hands of your lady-love, and with the trumpets braying, and the populace shouting, and the Queen of Beauty smiling sweet approval on your prowess: but it is quite another thing to walk up and down a dusty country road, with the wind biting like some ravenous animal at the tip of your nose, and no more consciousness of your legs and arms than if you were a Miss Biffin.

By the time seven o'clock struck, Clement Austin's patience had given up the ghost; and to impatience had succeeded a vague sense of alarm. Margaret Wilmot had gone to force herself into this man's presence, in spite of his reiterated refusal to see her. What if—what if, goaded by her persistence, maddened by the consciousness of his own guilt, he should attempt any violence?

Oh, no, no; that was quite impossible. If this man was guilty, his crime had been deliberately planned; and executed with such a diabolical cunning, that he had been able so far to escape detection. In his own house, surrounded by prying servants, he would never dare to assail this girl by so much as a harsh word.

But notwithstanding this, Clement was determined to wait no longer. He would go to the Abbey at once, and ascertain the cause of Margaret's delay. He rang the bell, went into the park, and ran along the avenue to the porch. Lights were shining in Mr. Dunbar's windows, but the great hall-door was closely shut.

The languid footman came in answer to Clement's summons.

"There is a young lady here," Clement said, breathlessly; "a young lady—with Mr. Dunbar."

"Ho! is that hall?" asked the footman, satirically. "I thought Shorncliffe town-'all was a-fire, at the very least, from the way you rung. There *was* a young pusson with Mr. Dunbar above a hour ago, if *that*'s what you mean?"

"Above an hour ago?" cried Clement Austin, heedless of the man's impertinence in his own growing anxiety; "do you mean to say that the young lady has left?"

"She *have* left, above a hour ago."

"She went away from this house an hour ago?"

"More than a hour ago."

"Impossible!" Clement said; "impossible!"

"It may be so," answered the footman, who was of an ironical turn of mind; "but I let her out with my own hands, and I saw her go out with my own eyes, notwithstanding."

The man shut the door before Clement had recovered from his surprise, and left him standing in the porch; bewildered, though he scarcely knew why; frightened, though he scarcely knew what he feared.

CHAPTER XVI.

MARGARET'S RETURN.

FOR some minutes Clement Austin lingered in the porch at Maudesley Abbey, utterly at a loss as to what he should do next.

Margaret had left the Abbey an hour ago, according to the footman's statement; but, in that case, where had she gone? Clement had been walking up and down the road before the iron gates of the park, and they had not been opened once during the hours in which he had waited outside them. Margaret could not have left the park, therefore, by the principal entrance. If she had gone away at all, she must have gone out by one of the smaller gates—by the lodge-gate upon the Lisford Road perhaps, and thus back to Shorncliffe.

But then, why, in Heaven's name, had Margaret set out to walk home when the fly was waiting for her at the gates; when her lover was also waiting for her, full of anxiety to know the result of the step she had taken?

"She forgot that I was waiting for her, perhaps," Clement thought to himself. "She may have forgotten all about me, in the fearful excitement of this night's work."

The young man was by no means pleased by this idea.

"Margaret can love me very little, in that case," he said to himself. "My first thought, in any great crisis of my life, would be to go to her, and tell her all that had happened to me."

There were no less than four different means of exit from the park. Clement Austin knew this, and he knew that it would take him upwards of two hours to go to all four of them.

"I'll make inquiries at the gate upon the Lisford Road," he said to himself; "and if I find Margaret has left by that way, I can get the fly round there, and pick her up between this and Shorncliffe. Poor girl, in her ignorance of this neighbourhood, she has no idea of the distance she will have to walk!"

Mr. Austin could not help feeling vexed by Margaret's conduct; but he did all he could to save the girl from the fatigue she was likely to entail upon herself through her own folly. He ran to the lodge upon the Lisford Road, and asked the woman who kept it, if a lady had gone out about an hour before.

The woman told him that a young lady had gone out an hour and a half before.

This was enough. Clement ran across the park to the western entrance, got into the fly, and told the man to drive back to Shorncliffe, by the Lisford Road, as fast as he could go, and to look out on the way for the young lady whom he had driven to Maudesley Abbey that afternoon.

"You watch the left side of the road, I'll watch the right," Clement said.

The driver was cold and cross, but he was anxious to get back to Shorncliffe, and he drove very fast.

Clement sat with the window down, and the

frosty wind blowing full upon his face as he looked out for Margaret.

But he reached Shorncliffe without having overtaken her, and the fly crawled under the ponderous archway beneath which the dashing mail-coaches had rolled in the days that were for ever gone.

"She must have got home before me," the cashier thought; "I shall find her upstairs with my mother."

He went up to the large room with the bow-window. The table in the centre of the room was laid for dinner, and Mrs. Austin was nodding in a great arm-chair near the fire, with the county newspaper in her lap. The wax-candles were lighted, the crimson curtains were drawn before the bow-window, and the room looked altogether very comfortable: but there was no Margaret.

The widow started up at the sound of the opening of the door and her son's hurried footsteps.

"Why, Clement," she cried, "how late you are! I seem to have been sitting dozing here for full two hours; and the fire has been replenished three times since the cloth was laid for dinner. What have you been doing, my dear boy?"

Clement looked about him before he answered.

"Yes, I am very late, mother, I know," he said; "but where's Margaret?"

Mrs. Austin stared aghast at her son's question.

"Why, Margaret is with you, is she not?" she exclaimed.

"No, mother; I expected to find her here."

"Did you leave her, then?"

"No, not exactly; that is to say, I—"

Clement did not finish the sentence. He walked slowly up and down the room thinking, while his mother watched him very anxiously.

"My dear Clement," Mrs. Austin exclaimed at last, "you really quite alarm me. You set out this afternoon upon some mysterious expedition with Margaret; and though I ask you both where you are going, you both refuse to satisfy my very natural curiosity, and look as solemn as if you were about to attend a funeral. Then, after ordering dinner for seven o'clock, you keep it waiting nearly two hours; and you come in without Margaret, and seem alarmed at not seeing her here. What does it all mean, Clement?"

"I cannot tell you, mother."

"What! is this business of to-day a part of your secret?"

"It is," answered the cashier. "I can only say again what I said before, mother—trust me!"

The widow sighed, and shrugged her shoulders with a deprecating gesture.

"I suppose I *must* be satisfied, Clem," she said. "But this is the first time there's ever been any thing like a mystery between you and me."

"It is, mother; and I hope it may be the last."

The elderly waiter, who remembered the coaching days, and pretended to believe that the Reindeer was not an institution of the past, came in presently with the first course.

It happened to be one of those days on which fish was to be had in Shorncliffe; and the first course consisted of a pair of very small soles and a large cruet-stand. The waiter removed the cover with as lofty a flourish as if the small soles had been the noblest turbot that ever made the glory of an aldermanic feast.

Clement seated himself at the dinner-table, in deference to his mother, and went through the ceremony of dinner; but he scarcely ate half a dozen mouthfuls. His ears were strained to hear the sound of Margaret's footstep in the corridor without; and he rejected the waiter's fish-sauces in a manner that almost wounded the feelings of that functionary. His mind was racked by anxiety about the missing girl.

Had he passed her on the road? No, that was very improbable; for he had kept so sharp a watch upon the lonely highway that it was more than unlikely the familiar figure of her whom he looked for could have escaped his eager eyes. Had Mr. Dunbar detained her at Maudesley Abbey against her will? No, no, that was quite impossible; for the footman had distinctly declared that he had seen his master's visitor leave the house; and the footman's manner had been innocence itself.

The dinner-table was cleared by and by, and Mrs. Austin produced some coloured wools, and a pair of ivory knitting-needles, and set to work very quietly by the light of the tall wax-candles; but even she was beginning to be uneasy at the absence of her son's betrothed wife.

"My dear Clement," she said at last, "I'm really growing quite uneasy about Madge. How is it that you left her?"

Clement did not answer this question; but he got up and took his hat from a side-table near the door.

"I'm uneasy about her absence too, mother," he said. "I'll go and look for her."

He was leaving the room, but his mother called to him.

"Clement!" she cried, "you surely won't go out without your greatcoat—upon such a bitter night as this, too!"

But Mr. Austin did not stop to listen to his mother's remonstrance; he hurried out into the corridor, and shut the door of the room behind him. He wanted to run away and look for Margaret, though he did not know how or where to seek for her. Quiescence had become intolerable to him. It was utterly impossible that he should sit calmly by the fire, waiting for the coming of the girl he loved.

He was hurrying along the corridor, but he stopped abruptly: for a well-known figure appeared upon the broad landing at the top of the stairs. There was an archway at the end of the corridor, and a lamp hung under the archway. By the light of this lamp, Clement Austin saw Margaret Wilmot coming towards him slowly: as if she dragged herself along by a painful effort, and would have been well content to sink upon the carpeted floor, and lie there helpless and inert.

Clement ran to meet her, with his face lighted up by that intense delight which a man feels when some intolerable fear is suddenly lifted off his mind.

"Margaret!" he cried; "thank God you have returned! Oh, my dear, if you only knew what misery your conduct has caused me!"

He held out his arms, but, to his unutterable surprise, the girl recoiled from him. She recoiled from him with a look of horror, and shrank against the wall, as if her chief desire was to avoid the slightest contact with her lover.

Clement was startled by the blank whiteness of her face, the fixed stare of her dilated eyes. The January wind had blown her hair about her forehead in loose disordered tresses; her shawl and dress were wet with melted snow; but the cashier scarcely looked at these. He only saw her face; his gaze was fascinated by the girl's awful pallor, and the strange expression of her eyes.

"My darling," he said, "come into the parlour. My mother has been almost as much alarmed as I have been. Come, Margaret; my poor girl, I can see that this interview has been too much for you. Come, dear."

Once more he approached her, and again she shrank away from him, dragging herself along against the wall, and with her eyes still fixed in the same deathlike stare.

"Don't speak to me, Clement Austin," she cried; "don't approach me. There is contamination in me. I am no fit associate for an honest man. Don't come near me."

He would have gone to her, to clasp her in his arms, and comfort her with soothing, tender words; but there was something in her eyes that held him at bay, as if he had been rooted to the spot on which he stood.

"Margaret!" he cried.

He followed her, but she still recoiled from him, and, as he held out his hand to grasp her wrist, she slipped by him suddenly, and rushed away towards the other end of the corridor.

Clement followed her; but she opened a door at the end of the passage, and went into Mrs. Austin's room. The cashier heard the key turned hurriedly in the lock, and he knew that Margaret Wilmot had locked herself in. The room in which she slept was inside that occupied by Mrs. Austin.

Clement stood for some moments almost paralysed by what had happened. Had he done wrong in seeking to bring about this interview between Margaret Wilmot and Henry Dunbar? He began to think that he had been most culpable. This impulsive and sensitive girl had seen her father's assassin: and the horror of the meeting had been too much for her impressionable nature, and had produced, for the time at least, a fearful effect upon her over-wrought brain.

"I must appeal to my mother," Clement thought; "she alone can give me any help in this business."

He hurried back to the sitting-room, and found his mother still watching the rapid movements of her ivory knitting-needles. The Reindeer was a well-built house, solid and old-fashioned, and listeners lurking in the long passages had small chance of reaping much reward for their pains, unless they found a friendly keyhole.

Mrs. Austin looked up with an expression of surprise as her son reëntered the room.

"I thought you had gone to look for Margaret?" she said.

"There was no occasion to do so, mother; she has returned."

"Thank heaven for that! I have been quite alarmed by her strange absence."

"So have I, mother; but I am still more alarmed by her manner, now that she has returned.

I asked you just now to trust me, mother," said Clement, very gravely. "It is my turn now to confide in you. The business in which Margaret has been engaged this evening was of a most painful nature—so painful that I am scarcely surprised by the effect that it has produced on her sensitive mind. I want you to go to her, mother. I want you to comfort my poor girl. She has locked herself in her own room; but she will admit you, no doubt. Go to her, dear mother, and try and quiet her excitement, while I go for a medical man."

"You think she is ill, then, Clement?"

"I don't know that, mother; but such violent emotion as she has evidently endured might produce brain-fever. I'll go and look for a doctor."

Clement hurried down to the hall of the hotel, while his mother went to seek Margaret. He found the landlord, who directed him to the favourite Shorncliffe medical man.

Luckily, Mr. Vincent the surgeon was at home. He received Clement very cordially, put on his hat without five minutes' delay, and accompanied Margaret's lover back to the Reindeer.

"It is a case of mental excitement," Clement said. "There may be no necessity for medical treatment; but I shall feel more comfortable when you have seen this poor girl."

Clement conducted Mr. Vincent to the sitting-room, which was empty.

"I'll go and see how Miss Wilmot is now," the cashier said.

The doctor gave a scarcely perceptible start as he heard that name of Wilmot. The murder of Joseph Wilmot had formed the subject of many a long discussion amongst the townspeople at Shorncliffe, and the familiar name struck the surgeon's ear.

"But what of that?" thought Mr. Vincent. "The name is not such a very uncommon one."

Clement went to his mother's room, and knocked softly at the door. The widow came out to him presently.

"How is she now?" Clement asked.

"I can scarcely tell you. Her manner frightens

me. She is lying on her bed as motionless as if she were a corpse, and with her eyes fixed upon the blank wall opposite to her. When I speak to her, she does not answer me by so much as a look; but if I go near her, she shivers, and gives a long shuddering sigh. What does it all mean, Clement?"

"Heaven knows, mother. I can only tell you that she has gone through a meeting which was certainly calculated to have considerable effect upon her mind. But I had no idea that the effect would be any thing like this. Can the doctor come?"

"Yes; he had better come at once."

Clement returned to the sitting-room, and remained there while Mr. Vincent went to see Margaret. To poor Clement it seemed as if the surgeon was absent nearly an hour, so intolerable was the anguish of that interval of suspense.

At last, however, the creaking footstep of the medical man sounded in the corridor. Clement hurried to the door to meet him.

"Well!" he cried, eagerly.

Mr. Vincent shook his head.

"It is a case in which my services can be of very little avail," he said; "the young lady is suffering from some mental uneasiness, which she refuses to communicate to her friends. If you could get her to talk to you, she would no doubt be very much benefited. If she were an ordinary person, she would cry, and the relief of tears would have a most advantageous effect upon her mind. Our patient is by no means an ordinary person. She has a very strong will."

"Margaret has a strong will!" exclaimed Clement, with a look of surprise; "why, she is gentleness itself."

"Very likely; but she has a will of iron, nevertheless. I implored her to speak to me just now; the tone of her voice would have been some slight diagnosis of her state; but I might as well have implored a statue. She only shook her head slowly, and she never once looked at me. However, I will send her a sedative draught, which had better be taken immediately, and I'll look round in the morning."

Mr. Vincent left the Reindeer, and Clement

went to his mother's room. That loving mother was ready to sympathise with every trouble that affected her only son. She came out of Margaret's room, and went to meet Clement.

"Is she still the same, mother?" he asked.

"Yes, quite the same. Would you like to see her?"

"Very much."

Mrs. Austin and her son went into the adjoining chamber.

Margaret was lying, dressed in the damp, draggled gown which she had worn that afternoon, upon the outside of the bed. The dull stony look of her face filled Clement's mind with an awful terror. He began to fear that she was going mad.

He sat down upon a chair close by the bed, and watched her for some moments in silence, while his mother stood by, scarcely less anxious than himself.

Margaret's arm hung loosely by her side, as lifeless in its attitude as if it had belonged to the dead. Clement took the slender hand in his. He had expected to find it dry and burning with feverish heat; but, to his surprise, it was cold as ice.

"Margaret," he said, in a low earnest voice, "you know how dearly I have loved and do love you; you know how entirely my happiness depends upon yours; surely, my dear one, you will not refuse—you cannot be so cruel as to keep your sorrow a secret from him who has so good a right to share it? Speak to me, my darling. Remember what suffering you are inflicting upon me by this cruel silence."

At last the hazel eyes lost their fixed look, and wandered for a moment to Clement Austin's face.

"Have pity upon *me*," the girl said, in a hoarse, unnatural voice; "have compassion upon *me*, for I need man's mercy as well as the mercy of God. Have some pity upon me, Clement Austin, and leave me; I will talk to you to-morrow."

"You will tell me all that has happened?"

"I will talk to you to-morrow," answered Margaret, looking at her lover with a white, inflexible face; "but leave me now; leave me, or I will run out of this room, and away from this house. I shall go mad if I am not left alone!"

Clement Austin rose from his seat near the bedside.

"I am going, Margaret," he said, in a tone of wounded feeling; "but I leave you with a heavy heart. I did not think there would ever come a time in which you would reject my sympathy."

"I will talk to you to-morrow," Margaret said, for the third time.

She spoke in a strange mechanical way, as if this bad been a set speech which she had arranged for herself.

Clement stood looking at her for some little time; but there was no change either in her face or attitude, and the young man went slowly and sorrowfully from the room.

"I leave her in your hands, mother," he said. "I know how tender and true a friend she has in you; I leave her in your care, under Providence. May Heaven have pity upon her and me!"

CHAPTER XVII.

FAREWELL.

MARGARET submitted to take the sedative draught sent by the medical man. She submitted, at Mrs. Austin's request; but it seemed as if she scarcely understood why the medicine was offered to her. She was like a sleep-walker, whose brain is peopled by the creatures of a dream, and who has no consciousness of the substantial realities that surround him.

The draught, which Mr. Vincent had spoken of as a sedative, turned out to be a very powerful opiate, and Margaret sank into a profound slumber about a quarter of an hour after taking the medicine.

Mrs. Austin went to Clement to carry him these good tidings.

"I shall sit up two or three hours, and see

how the poor girl goes on, Clement," the widow said; "but I hope you'll go to bed; I know all this excitement has worn you out."

"No, mother; I feel no sense of fatigue."

"But you will try to get some rest, to please me? See, dear boy, it's already nearly twelve o'clock!"

"Yes, if you wish it, mother, I'll go to my room," Mr. Austin answered, quickly.

His room was near those occupied by his mother and Margaret, much nearer than the sitting-room. He bade Mrs. Austin good night and left her; but he had no thought of going to bed, or even trying to sleep. He went to his own room, and walked up and down; going out into the corridor every now and then, to listen at the door of his mother's chamber.

He heard nothing. Some time between two and three o'clock Mrs. Austin opened the door of her room, and found her son lingering in the corridor.

"Is she still asleep, mother?" he asked.

"Yes, and she is sleeping very calmly. I am

going to bed now; pray try to get some sleep yourself, Clem."

"I will, mother."

Clement returned to his room. He was thankful, as he thought that sleep would bring tranquillity and relief to Margaret's over-wrought brain. He went to bed and fell asleep, for he was exhausted by the fatigue of the day and the anxiety of the night. Poor Clement fell asleep, and dreamt that he met Margaret Wilmot by moonlight in the park around Maudesley Abbey, walking with a DEAD MAN, whose face was strange to him. This was the last of many dreams, all more or less grotesque or horrible, but none so vivid or distinct as this. The end of the vision woke Clement with a sudden shock, and he opened his eyes upon the cold morning light; which seemed especially cold in this chamber at the Reindeer, where the paper on the walls was of the palest gray, and every curtain or drapery of a spotless white.

Clement lost no time over his toilet. He looked at his watch while dressing, and found that it was between seven and eight. It wanted a quarter to eight when he left his room, and went to his mother's door to inquire about Margaret. He knocked softly, but there was no answer; then he tried the door, and finding it unlocked, opened it a few inches with a cautious hand, and listened to his mother's regular breathing.

"She is asleep, poor soul," he thought. "I won't disturb her, for she must want rest after sitting up half last night."

Clement closed the door as noiselessly as he had opened it, and then went slowly to the sitting-room. There was a struggling fire in the shining grate; and the indefatigable waiter, who refused to believe in the extinction of mail-coaches, had laid the breakfast apparatus—frosty-looking white-and-blue cups and saucers on a snowy cloth, a cut-glass cream-jug that looked as if it had been made out of ice, and a brazen urn in the last stage of polish. The breakfast-service was harmoniously adapted to the season, and eminently calculated to produce a fit of shivering in the sojourner at the Reindeer.

But Clement Austin did not bestow so much as one glance upon the breakfast-table. He hurried to the bow-window, where Margaret Wilmot was sitting, neatly dressed in her morning garments, with her shawl on, and her bonnet lying on a chair near her.

"Margaret," exclaimed Clement, as he approached the place where Joseph Wilmot's daughter was sitting; "my dear Margaret, why did you get up so early this morning, when you so much need rest?"

The girl rose and looked at her lover with a grave and quiet earnestness of expression; but her face was quite as colourless as it had been upon the previous night, and her lips trembled a little as she spoke to Clement.

"I have had sufficient rest," she said, in a low, tremulous voice; "I got up early because—because—I am going away."

Her two hands had been hanging loosely amongst the fringes of her shawl; she lifted them now, and linked her fingers together with a convulsive motion; but she never withdrew her eyes from Clement's face, and her glance never faltered as she looked at him.

"Going away, Margaret?" the cashier cried; "going away—to-day—this morning?"

"Yes, by the half-past nine o'clock train."

"Margaret, you must be mad to talk of such a thing."

"No," the girl answered slowly; "that is the strangest thing of all—I am not mad. I am going away, Clement—Mr. Austin. I wished to avoid seeing you. I meant to have written to you to tell you—"

"To tell me what, Margaret?" asked Clement. "Is it I who am going mad; or am I dreaming all this?"

"It is no dream, Mr. Austin. My letter would have only told you the truth. I am going away from here because I can never be your wife."

"You can never be my wife! Why not, Margaret?"

"I cannot tell you the reason."

"But you *shall* tell me, Margaret!" cried Clement, passionately. "I will accept no sentence such as this until I know your reason for pronouncing it; I will suffer no imaginary barrier to stand between you and me. There is some mystery, some mystification in all this, Margaret; some woman's fancy, which a few words of explanation would set at rest. Margaret, my pearl! do you think I will consent to lose you so lightly? My own dear love! do you know me so little as to think that I will part with you? My love is a stronger passion than you think, Madge; and the bondage you accepted when you promised to be my wife is a bondage that cannot so easily be shaken off!"

Margaret watched her lover's face with melancholy, tearless eyes.

"Fate is stronger than love, Clement," she said, mournfully. "I can never be your wife!"

"Why not?"

"For a reason which you can never know."

"Margaret, I will not submit—"

"You must submit," the girl said, holding up her hand, as if to stop her lover's passionate words. "You must submit, Clement. This world seems very hard sometimes, so hard that in a dreadful interval of dull despair the heavens are hidden from us, and we cannot recognise the Eternal wisdom guiding the hand that afflicts us. My life seems very hard to me to-day, Clement. Do not try to make it harder. I am a most unhappy woman; and in all the world there is only one favour you can grant me. Let me go away unquestioned; and blot my image from your heart for ever when I am gone."

"I will never consent to let you go," Clement Austin answered resolutely. "You are mine by right of your own most sacred promise, Margaret. No womanish folly shall part us."

"Heaven knows it is no woman's folly that parts us, Clement," the girl answered, in a plaintive, tremulous voice.

"What is it, then, Margaret?"

"I can never tell you."

"You will change your mind."

"Never."

She looked at him with an air of quiet resolution stamped upon her colourless face.

Clement remembered what the doctor had said of his patient's iron will. Was it possible that Mr. Vincent had been right? Was this gentle girl's resolution to overrule a strong man's passionate vehemence.

"What is it that can part us, Margaret?" Mr. Austin cried. "What is it? You saw Mr. Dunbar yesterday?"

The girl shuddered, and over her colourless face there came a livid shade, which was more deathlike than the marble whiteness that had preceded it.

"Yes," Margaret Wilmot said, after a pause. "I was—very fortunate. I gained admission to —Mr. Dunbar's rooms."

"And you spoke to him?"

"Yes."

"Did your interview with him confirm or dissipate your suspicions? Do you still believe that Henry Dunbar murdered your unhappy father?'

"No," answered Margaret, resolutely; "I do not."

"You do not? The banker's manner convinced you of his innocence, then?"

"I do not believe that Henry Dunbar murdered my—my unhappy father."

It is impossible to describe the tone of anguish with which Margaret spoke those last three words.

"But something transpired in that interview at Maudesley Abbey, Margaret? Henry Dunbar told you something—perhaps something about your dead father—some disgraceful secret which you never heard before; and you think that the shame of that secret is a burden which I would fear to carry? You mistake my nature, Margaret, and you commit a cruel treason against my love. Be my wife, dear one; and if malicious people should point to you, and say, 'Clement Austin's wife is the daughter of a thief and a forger,' I would give them back scorn for scorn, and tell them that I honour my wife for virtues that have been sometimes missing in the consort of an emperor."

For the first time that morning Margaret's eyes grew dim, but she brushed away the gathering tears with a rapid movement of her trembling hand.

"You are a good man, Clement Austin," she said; "and I—I—wish that I were better worthy of you. You are a good man; but you are very cruel to me to-day. Have pity upon me, and let me go."

She drew a pretty little watch from her waist, and looked at the dial. Then, suddenly remembering that the watch had been Clement's gift, she took the slender chain from her neck, and handed them both to him.

"You gave me these when I was your betrothed wife, Mr. Austin; I have no right to keep them now."

She spoke very mournfully; but poor Clement was only mortal. He was a good man, as Margaret had just declared; but, unhappily, good men are apt to fly into passions as well as their inferiors in the scale of morality.

Clement Austin threw the pretty little Genevese toy upon the floor, and ground it to atoms under the heel of his boot.

"You are cruel and unjust, Mr. Austin," Margaret said.

"I am a man, Miss Wilmot," Clement answered, bitterly; "and I have the feelings of a man. When the woman I have loved and believed in turns upon me, and coolly tells me that she means to break my heart, without so much as deigning to give me a reason for her conduct, I am not so much a gentleman as to be able to smile politely, and request her to please herself."

The cashier turned away from Margaret, and walked two or three times up and down the room. He was in a passion, but grief and indignation were so intermingled in his breast that he scarcely knew which was uppermost. But grief and love allied themselves presently, and together were much too strong for indignation.

Clement Austin went back to the window; Margaret was standing where he had left her, but she had put on her bonnet and gloves, and was quite ready to leave the house.

"Margaret," said Mr. Austin, trying to take

her hand; but she drew herself away from him, almost as she had shrunk from him in the corridor on the previous night; "Margaret, once for all, listen to me. I love you, and I believe that you love me. If this is true, no obstacle on earth shall part us so long as we live. There is only one condition upon which I will let you go this day."

"What is that condition?"

"Tell me that I have been fooled by my own egotism. I am twelve years older than you, Margaret, and there is nothing very romantic or interesting either in myself or my worldly position. Tell me that you do not love me. I am a proud man. I will not sue *in formâ pauperis.* If you do not love me, Margaret, you are free to go."

Margaret bowed her head, and moved slowly towards the door.

"You are going—Miss Wilmot!"

"Yes, I am going. Farewell, Mr. Austin."

Clement caught the retreating girl by her wrist.

"You shall not go thus, Margaret Wilmot!" he cried, passionately—"not thus! You shall speak to me! You shall speak plainly! You shall speak the truth! You do not love me?"

"No; I do not love you."

"It was all a farce, then—a delusion—it was all falsehood and trickery from first to last. When you smiled at me, your smile was a mockery; when you blushed, your blushes were the simulated blushes of a professed coquette. Every tender word you have ever spoken to me—every tremulous cadence in your low voice—every tearful look in the eyes that have seemed so truthful—all—it has altogether been false—altogether a delusion—a—"

The strong man covered his face with his hands and sobbed aloud. Margaret watched him with tearless eyes; her lips were convulsively contracted, but there was no other evidence of emotion in her face.

"Why did you do this, Margaret?" Clement asked at last, in a heart-rending voice; "why did you do this cruel thing?"

"I will tell you why," the girl answered, slowly and deliberately; "I will tell you why,

Mr. Austin; and then I shall seem utterly despicable in your eyes, and it will be a very easy thing for you to blot my image from your heart. I was a poor desolate girl; and I was worse than poor and desolate, for the stain of my father's shameful history blackened my name. It was a fine thing for such as me to win the love of an honest man—a gentleman—who could shelter me from all the troubles of life, and give me a stainless name and an honourable place in society. I was the daughter of a returned convict, an outcast, and your love offered me a splendid chance of redemption from the black depths of disgrace and misery in which I lived. I was only mortal, Clement Austin; what was there in my blood that should make me noble, or good, or strong to stand against temptation? I seized upon the one chance of my miserable life; I plotted to win your love. Step by step I lured you on until you offered to make me your wife. That was my end and aim. I triumphed; and for a time enjoyed my success, and the advantages that it brought me. But I suppose the worst sinners have some kind of conscience. Mine was awakened last night, and I resolved to spare you the misery of being married to a woman who comes of such a race as that from which I spring."

Nothing could be more callous than the manner with which Margaret Wilmot had made this speech. Her tones had never faltered. She had spoken slowly, pausing before every fresh sentence; but she had spoken like a wretched creature, whose withered heart was almost incapable of womanly emotion.

Clement Austin looked at her with a blank, wondering stare.

"Oh! great heavens!" he cried at last; "how could I think it possible that any man could be as cruelly deceived as I have been by this woman!"

"I may go now, Mr. Austin?" said Margaret.

"Yes, you may go now—*you*, who once were the woman I loved; you, who have thrown away the beautiful mask I believed in, and revealed to me the face of a skeleton; you, who have lifted the silver veil of imagination to show me the hideous ghastliness of reality. Go, Margaret Wilmot; and may Heaven forgive you!"

"Do you forgive me, Mr. Austin?"

"Not yet. I will pray God to make me strong enough to forgive you!"

"Farewell, Clement."

If my readers have seen *Manfred* at Drury Lane, let them remember the tone in which Miss Rose Leclercq breathed her last farewell to Mr. Phelps, and they will know how Margaret Wilmot pronounced this mournful word—love's funeral bell—

"Farewell, Clement."

"One word, Miss Wilmot," cried Mr. Austin. "I have loved you too much in the past ever to become indifferent to your fate. Where are you going?"

"To London."

"To your old apartments at Clapham?"

"Oh, no, no!"

"Have you money—money enough to last you for some time?"

"Yes; I have saved some money."

"If you should be in want of help, will you let me help you?"

"Willingly, Mr. Austin. I am not too proud to accept your help in the hour of my need."

"You will write to me, then, at my mother's, or you will write to my mother herself, if ever you require assistance. I shall tell my mother nothing of what has passed between us this day, except that we have parted. You are going by the half-past nine o'clock train, you say, Miss Wilmot?"

Clement had only spoken the truth when he said that he was a proud man. He asked this question in the same business-like tone in which he might have addressed a lady who was quite indifferent to him.

"Yes, Mr. Austin."

"I will order a fly for you, then. You have five minutes to spare. And I will send one of the waiters to the station, so that you may have no trouble about your luggage."

Clement rang the bell, and gave the necessary

orders. Then he bowed gravely to Margaret, and wished her good morning as she left the room.

And this is how Margaret Wilmot parted from Clement Austin.

END OF VOL. II.

CPSIA information can be obtained
at www.ICGtesting.com
Printed in the USA
LVHW040026180422
716440LV00005B/396

9 783752 593969